WITCH HAUNTED IN WESTERHAM

Paranormal Investigation Bureau Book 7

DIONNE LISTER

To my loyal readers, knowing you're out there reading my books brings me all the joy. Thank you for walking alongside me on this journey.

CHAPTER 1

I clenched my stomach, gritted my teeth, and strained. Sweat popped out on my forehead. This was way harder than it was supposed to be.

"You can do it, Lily. Come on. You almost had it!" I appreciated Imani's encouragement, but it didn't make this any easier.

As I grunted and pushed one more time, I wondered if there was a magic-related equivalent of haemorrhoids because if there was, I was sure to have it after this. A pulse of warmth floated up from my stomach and out through my fingers. The candle wick ignited into a small but real flame.

"Woohoo!" Olivia jumped up, fists in the air, victorious. "You did it!"

I slumped back on the Chesterfield, exhausted, but I smiled. It had taken three weeks to get to this point. Tonight couldn't have come soon enough, really. After almost dying and having to just about burn my magic out to save myself from Jeremy's evil mother, I was sure I would never get my magic back. But it was still there. My smile widened.

Imani patted my knee. "You did it, love. Brilliant." She and Olivia grinned at me, and was that a tear in Liv's eye?

"Thanks, ladies. I would've given up by now if it weren't for you. This hasn't been easy." They both knew I was talking about more than the magic. I hadn't seen or heard from Will since before I'd been kidnapped. Our fake break-up was all too real. He'd been deep undercover the past three weeks, and if it wasn't for Angelica's periodical updates, he could've been dead, for all I knew. That, combined with my lack of being able to access my magic, had kept me in my room moping most of the time, although I preferred to think of it as "resting."

"This calls for a celebration." Imani waved, and three cups of hot chocolate appeared on the table between the Chesterfields. She grabbed two, passing one to me. "You've earned it."

I hovered my nose over the cup and inhaled. Mmm, chocolate. I sipped the richly sweet beverage, savouring the taste, then the warmth as it slid down my throat. "Thanks, Imani. I didn't think I'd ever get my magic back." I shivered. There were times since I'd arrived in the UK that I thought my magic was more trouble than it was worth, but after everything that had happened, I knew losing it would leave a hole inside me forever. It wouldn't be as bad as missing my parents, but it would come a close second, although I would give up my magic to have my parents back. I sat up straight. What if they were hidden some-where, and all it would take was telling Dana Piranha that she could have my magic to get them back?

Olivia's brow wrinkled. "What is it, Lily?"

"Do either of you think my parents might still be alive?" The sad looks they both gave me had me regretting the question. I sighed.

"Sorry, love. But you know we'll get to the bottom of what happened. I won't stop looking till we do."

"Me neither." I placed my cup on the table and looked at each of them in turn. "What would I do without you two?"

"You'll never have to find out." Liv grinned.

"Never." Imani gave a nod.

"I can live with that."

"How are you feeling after that?" Imani asked.

"Exhausted but happy. I reckon I could sleep for twelve hours. Thirty minutes of straining was more than enough."

"Next, we'll be getting you a walking frame." Olivia laughed.

"Don't laugh. I feel like this near-death thing aged me twenty years."

Bang. Bang. Bang! Either someone really needed to borrow a cup of sugar, or it was a police raid because whoever was out there was about to smash the door down with their enthusiasm.

"Are you expecting anyone?" Olivia looked at me.

"No. Are you?"

She shook her head. "I'll get it. You stay there and rest, Gran." She winked.

"Yeah, yeah, have your fun, but when I'm at full strength again, I'll turn you into a dung beetle for a day."

Her eyes widened in horror. *Thump*! *Thump*! *Thump*! She gave me one last desperate look, then hurried to answer the door. Indistinct voices floated in. The door clunked shut, and Olivia led a shocked-looking old lady into the room—Mrs Soames from across the road. She shuffled towards the Chesterfields, one hand on her heart. Olivia helped her settle into the couch opposite me and asked, "Would you like a hot chocolate or cup of tea, Mrs Soames?"

She blinked, her expression still set to stunned. What had happened? Her voice was shaky. "Ah, yes, love. Yes. I think that would be good. Thank you."

Olivia smiled and left the room to make the tea the normal way. Our neighbour wasn't a witch, and seeing as how she was already put out about something, witnessing magic would probably do her in.

I asked gently, "What's wrong, Mrs Soames? You look as if you've seen a ghost. Are you okay? Do you need us to call an ambulance?" Maybe she'd had chest pains, and it had frightened her.

"Well, actually, as I was just explaining to Olivia, I *have* just seen a ghost." She shook her head and hugged herself. "Crazy, I know, but still…."

I didn't want to be rude, but my eyebrows crept up in disbelief. It was an out-there claim. Okay, so witches were too, yet here I was…. "How do you know it was a ghost? Maybe it was a shadow or something?"

She shook her head emphatically. "No, no. I know what I saw. I may be old, but I'm not blind. It was a man I didn't know. He was bald and fat and had only trousers on." She shuddered. "He told me to get out of his house. I started to tell him that it was my house, that I'd lived there for forty years, when he opened his mouth and roared—a godawful sound that chilled my old bones. Horrid. Absolutely horrid. I stood up and left as fast as I could. As I left, he said not to come back. That if I did, I was dead."

Imani leaned forward. "Is this the first time you've ever seen a ghost, Mrs Soames?"

She muttered, "Manners," so quietly, I almost didn't hear it. She raised her volume to normal speaking level. "What's your name, if you don't mind?"

"Oh, sorry. I'm Imani. Lovely to meet you."

"She's a close friend of ours and works with Angelica," I supplied. Mrs Soames was shaken enough already, and I wanted to hear the rest of the story. Having her clam up was not going to help us get to the bottom of anything.

She nodded. "All right, that's good. Well, for the past week, I've been hearing noises—banging kitchen cupboard doors, footsteps, creaking floorboards. But it was always one or two sounds; then it would go quiet, making me wonder if I'd really heard anything. And yesterday, I lost my purse, and I never lose my purse. I found it in the bathtub, which is a ridiculous place to find it. Why would I put it there, I asked myself? Unless I've started sleepwalking, it had to have been the ghost. Then tonight, well, he appeared out of nowhere when I was watching a lovely David Attenborough documentary on Borneo." She took a deep breath and sunk back into the lounge with the out breath. She was on the short side, and her feet left the floor when she settled her back against the furniture.

Olivia walked in and set a tray with a teapot, cup, and accoutrements on the table, and poured a cup of tea for Mrs Soames. Was the old lady just losing it, or had something weird really happened?

Mrs Soames poured a dash of milk into her cup and took a sip, her hand trembling—with age or fear, I had no idea. She looked at Olivia, who sat beside her. "Thanks, love. Not enough young ones have proper manners these days." She flicked her gaze to Imani, just long enough for us to notice. Passive aggressive much?

Olivia smiled awkwardly through her surprise. "My pleasure." Liv turned to me and tipped her chin, silently asking me to figure out what to do. Why was this my call? I was tired, and my brain wasn't working as well as it normally did. I didn't feel like creeping through a haunted house, even though I didn't believe in ghosts. I was living proof that the unreal was real, and I didn't need any extra excitement tonight. *Ah, but there's always a solution, if you just think hard enough.*

I smiled at Mrs Soames. "Why don't Olivia and Imani go and see if the ghost is still there while I stay here and make sure you're safe?" Olivia tilted her head to the side with a "you have got to be kidding me" expression on her face, and Imani raised a brow. "What? I've been sick. I'm not up to seeing ghosts." As slack as I was being, what I said was true. I really wasn't up to anything right now, or maybe ever.

"Have you been sick, Lily?" Mrs Soames asked.

I nodded. "Yes. It's made me very tired. I've spent most of the last three weeks in bed."

"You look all right now, and to be honest, I'd rather not catch what you've had. I'd feel better if Olivia stayed with me." She patted Olivia's hand. Oh, brother. *Thanks, Mrs Soames.* She wanted me to go out in the cold and potentially get sicker—well, she didn't know what I'd had—just to save herself. She'd obviously had a good life. Why should I be sacrificed?

"Come on, Lily. I'll protect you." Imani smirked.

I narrowed my eyes. "Yeah, well, I need protecting right now. You know I can't protect myself." I frowned, and she dropped her smirk. Good, she felt as bad as I did. I rolled my eyes. "Let me go get rugged up. It's bloody freezing out there."

"Are you sure?" Ah, Olivia was having second thoughts, and so she should. I'd do what I had to, but they should at least suffer some guilt.

"Yeah, yeah. Looks like I've been outvoted." I trudged upstairs, put on my coat, beanie, and boots the normal way, and went back down. Not having magic for everyday things sucked. My room was going to be messy for a while. As long as Angelica didn't come in, I wouldn't get in trouble. Or maybe I could ask Imani to do a quick tidy with her magic.

We said goodbye and hurried across the street. "Yes, I'll tidy your room."

Oh, crap. My mind-shield wasn't up and hadn't been since I'd lost proper use of my powers. That was the other reason I'd avoided witchy people—having your thoughts there for all to see was embarrassing. I blushed. "Thanks. I'd appreciate it. I'd also appreciate it if you didn't read my mind."

"Hang on a sec." She put her hands on my cheeks, mumbled something, and my scalp tingled with warmth. She smiled. "Done. That should last a couple of days. I'll redo it then if you can't."

Gah, I shouldn't be angry at her. It wasn't Imani's fault, or Olivia's, that I was tired and lacking magical powers. I sighed. "Thank you. I'm sorry I've been so cranky. It's just…." I shut my mouth as tears burned the back of my throat. Missing my magic was hard enough, but not having Will around hurt the most. The longer the estrangement continued, the less chance we had of getting back to where we'd been—happy and slowly falling in love. Crap.

"Come on, Lily. You're shivering."

Oh, so I was. "Okay." I followed her to Mrs Soames's front porch. The front door of her neat brick bungalow was wide open. Anyone could have walked in and robbed her. She really must've been scared—she was an ordered person, and other than this ghost thing, always seemed to have her wits about her. Her garden was one of the prettiest in spring and summer, and she kept her home in pristine condition, if somewhat dated—her 1980s kitchen and bathroom didn't have a tile out of place.

We warily stepped into the hallway. "Do you believe in ghosts?" I whispered.

"Yes, of course."

"Then why aren't you whispering?" I kept my voice low. If there were ghosts, why announce we were coming?

She gave a short laugh. "Ghosts are nothing to fear. They can't actually do anything. I have a feeling she may have seen one, but there's no way it could've moved anything."

"Should we turn on the lights?" Call me crazy, but the lights were off, and there was supposedly a ghost lurking. I figured having the lights on was a smart call. Imani shrugged. That kind of apathy didn't help anyone. I made an executive decision and pulled the cord on the hallway light—ooh, antique light switches. The satisfying click reverberated up my fingers. How I'd missed that sensation. My grandparents in Sydney used to have these kinds of lights, and they'd also had a toilet with a chain you pulled to flush it. My brother and I used to pretend we were train drivers pulling the whistle on an old train. I smiled, but then melancholy slapped me in the side of the head. That's what you got for remembering the good times. Poop.

Imani confidently strode down the hallway, poking her head into one door, then another. She continued to the end of the corridor where a doorway opened into the living area. It must have been all clear so far since she hadn't said anything. After pausing, she flicked the light on and kept going.

I followed her into the living room, which had a six-seat timber dining table on one side, and a three-seat flower-print couch in front of a small TV. Half-eaten dinner sat on the table, a fork askew next to a plate. "Looks like the ghost interrupted her dinner." Imani didn't sound the least bit worried. She was a tougher woman than I.

Footsteps sounded from the hall. Olivia must have decided to join us. I turned around. Okay, so I couldn't have been more wrong. I sucked in a huge breath and held it, all my muscles tensed to run—I just needed to know which way the ghost was going to move; then I was gone.

A fat guy with no shirt hovered above the floor. He screamed, "Get out of my house!" flew at us in a rush of cold air and malevolence, and disappeared. My eyes were so wide, my eyelashes were just about stuck to my forehead. "What the ever-loving hell was that?" I mean, I knew it was the ghost, but still. Crap. My heart hammered, and I moved towards the hall and safety. "I'm leaving. You're welcome to stay, but I'm done. Mrs Soames can stay with us tonight. We have room."

Imani hurried past me but stopped in the spot we'd first seen the apparition. She whispered something, and I felt the tingle of magic, but then it stopped. "Hmm…." She folded her arms, then looked at me and shook her head. "I can't explain it. There isn't any trace of magic."

"You said ghosts existed, right? So it must be a ghost. We've confirmed what Mrs Soames told us. Now we can go." I squeezed past her and made it to the front door. I was not hanging around for visitation take two.

Imani sighed. "Yeah, well, we can't just leave it here to torment poor old Mrs Soames."

"Do you know how to banish ghosts?" I called from the front porch. One foot made it off the porch. With a bit of luck, I'd be across the road in no time.

"Lily, stop, for goodness' sake. Did it hurt you?" She put her hands on her hips.

"Ah, no. It stopped my heart a bit, but it's working again."

"Very funny. My point is, it can't hurt you, so stop being scared."

"Nuh-uh. Sorry, no can do. Can we just go now, please?"

She sighed dramatically and rolled her eyes. "You're such a baby."

"Am not."

"Are too."

"Am n—" Gah, she had me acting like a baby—well, maybe a three-year-old. "Do you know how to banish ghosts?"

"No, actually, I don't."

"So why in the hell would we wait around here for it to come back? It said to get out, and for once, I'm doing what I'm told." We all knew obedience wasn't my forte. Looked like I was growing as a person. Angelica would be pleased.

"Wait up." She shut the door, which was a good idea, although if the ghost was in there telling everyone to go away, I doubted a robber would last long enough to steal anything. She finally joined me on the kerb. We crossed the road and went home.

"You can tell her since you're the expert."

Imani rolled her eyes again. "I hardly know the lady. She's your neighbour," she whispered. I shrugged. What did that have to do with anything? As soon as we entered Angelica's lounge room, Olivia and Mrs Soames turned to us.

"Did you see it?" Olivia asked.

Imani and I looked at each other. She raised a brow. I huffed. "Fine." I hated being the bearer of bad news. I turned to Olivia and Mrs Soames. "There was definitely a ghost, and it was horrible—just as you described. We don't know how to get rid of it, though, so if you'd like to stay here tonight, you're welcome to."

"Oh, okay. Thank you, Lily." She stood. "I don't have any of my things."

"Do you think you'd be able to brave the ghost and go back with Imani? She's not scared at all. She can stay with you while you gather an overnight bag. She said ghosts can't hurt us, so I guess you'll be safe enough." I didn't envy Mrs Soames. I was never going back in that house again—I didn't care how many eyebrows Imani raised.

Mrs Soames paled. "I don't know if I can."

"It'll be fine. I promise." Imani stood next to Mrs Soames and hooked an arm through hers. "We'll do this together, and we won't take long. If the ghost screams at you again, just ignore him—he can't hurt you."

Mrs Soames took a deep breath and squared her shoulders. "Okay. I can do this. I'm eighty-five, dammit, and no ghost will keep me from gathering my things." She gave a firm nod and left with Imani.

Olivia looked at me. "Was there really a ghost?"

I nodded. "It was ugly, hairy, fat, cold, and very loud." I shuddered. "I never believed in ghosts, but now I know the truth. I'm not happy." I jerked my head around, feeling chilled and like someone was watching me. Olivia touched my shoulder, and I jumped. "Oh my God! Do not do that!"

She giggled. "Sorry, Lily. Wow, you really saw something, huh?"

I scrunched up my face and looked at her as if she was missing more than a slice from her loaf. "Seriously, Liv, what did I just say? I wasn't kidding."

She bit her bottom lip. "I'm sorry. I thought you were humouring her."

"Unfortunately, no. Ghosts exist. But why would one show up now when she's lived there for years with no dramas? It's weird." And there was no way I was going to sleep. Or maybe I'd keep my table lamp on tonight. Although the light in Mrs Soames's house hadn't stopped that ghost from appearing. What if he decided it wasn't fun to be in a house by himself with no one to scare, and he crossed the road to us? I grabbed my phone and dialled Angelica.

"Yes, dear?"

"Hi. Um, are you coming home soon?"

"I'll be home in about fifteen minutes. Why?"

"We have a guest staying the night—Mrs Soames from

across the road. I was just wondering if you could do a keep-ghosts-out spell."

"A what?"

"A keep-ghosts-out spell, you know, so no ghosts can come inside."

"There are no such things as ghosts, Lily. And why is Mrs Soames staying with us?"

"There's a ghost in her house, and it's ugly and noisy. Imani and I went over there and saw it for ourselves." I shuddered again.

"Right, Lily. I'll come home and set up one of the bedrooms on the first floor for Mrs Soames. I know you don't have your magic. Just sit tight. I'll be home soon."

"Thanks." I hung up as Imani and Mrs Soames came back through the door. The old lady carried her handbag and pillow, and Imani lugged a suitcase in one hand, and a huge covered birdcage in the other. Oh, that's right, Mrs Soames had an old cockatoo... a very loud cockatoo. This was going to be fun... not. And what if the ghost came here?

I explained that Angelica would be home soon, and that she'd make up a bed for Mrs Soames. After the monumental effort of magicking this afternoon and the horror of the ghost tonight, exhaustion bore down on me like a forty-kilo Marmaduke dog wanting a cuddle. I couldn't keep my eyes open. I bade everyone goodnight, and much to my happy surprise, I fell asleep as soon as I got into bed. Lucky for me because I was going to need it.

CHAPTER 2

A familiar prehistoric squawk woke me. It was more a shriek, really. The ear-splitting noise was the one thing I hadn't missed about Sydney. I cracked an eye open and checked my phone. 6:00 a.m. and still dark. Gah, give me a break. Morning number two was shaping up to be just as enjoyable as morning number one of having two house guests. I hadn't worked out who was less enjoyable to live with: Mrs Soames or her ornery cockatoo, Ethel.

I rolled over and pulled my covers tighter around me. Going back to sleep was the only thing I wanted to do right now. "Rawrk! Rawrk! Rawrk!" I lay on my stomach and held my pillow over my head. "Rawrk! Rawrk!" Nope, the noise still got through. And now there was knocking on my door.

I gave up and removed the pillow. "Yes, who is it?"

The door opened revealing a bright-eyed, bushy-tailed

Mrs Soames. Gah, I wasn't even safe in my room. I fought the urge to pull the covers over my head. "Lily, I can't find the tea. I didn't want to wake Angelica or Olivia—they work so hard. I know you slouch around the house all day."

And now the cockatoo screeching didn't seem so bad—it was just running on instinct; Mrs Soames, however…. I supposed I could just assume her attitude and not bother being polite. "Didn't I show you yesterday… three times?" Maybe she had dementia, and I shouldn't be so mean.

"Yes, but it's not where you showed me."

"Oh, sorry. I'll meet you in the kitchen in a minute." Well, didn't I feel like a horrible person. She shut my door, and I stumbled out of bed, still half asleep. I donned my dressing gown and Ugg boots—no reasonable person with nowhere to go would get dressed at this hour when there was a chance of going back to bed—and shuffled down to the kitchen.

You've got to be kidding. The only thing stopping me from committing murder right then was the all-too-fresh memory of being locked up in a PIB cell. Mrs Soames sat at the table with her wrinkly hands wrapped around a, you guessed it, fresh cup of tea. She smiled. "I found it!"

"She found it, rawrk. She found it."

I stared at the cockatoo, who stood on the table next to her cup. *Serenity now.* I had to thank *Seinfeld* and George for that little gem. The words made me think of the episode it came from and calmed me somewhat, although I was still heavily irritated. Grrr. "Of course she did." At least I didn't feel mean anymore. I promised myself not to ever get the guilts about being short with her again. She was doing this on purpose, I was sure, but I'd never be able to prove it.

I turned around and went back upstairs. Olivia was standing outside her room rubbing her eyes, her thick hair sticking up everywhere. "What's going on?"

"Our guest needed me to show her where the tea was, but then she found it herself."

Olivia rolled her eyes. "What a surprise."

"Yes, and you know how much I love those."

"Since we're both up, why don't we get dressed and grab something yummy at Costa?"

"I'm not really hungry, but I won't say no to a coffee. Oh, wait. I'll have to message Imani, and it's a bit early to be bothering her." After what happened to me with Jeremy's mother, and with Dana's group an ever-present danger, I wasn't allowed anywhere without protection again. And since I had only a smidgeon of magic, I was pretty much helpless. Imani had volunteered to protect me... with her life. Which was rather over the top, but she'd sworn it before anyone could stop her.

"She did say you could call her at any time of the day or night."

"I'm pretty sure she meant for emergencies. This is hardly an emergency."

"I beg to differ." Olivia giggled, and I smiled. She made a good point. Yesterday morning, after this same routine, Mrs Soames had gone to the TV room and put it on full blast. The voice vibrations and occasional cockatoo squawks stopped me from going back to sleep. I didn't know why I thought today would be any different. At least if I'd had magic, I could have put up some kind of silencing spell. "Remind me to ask Angelica to soundproof that TV room."

Olivia smiled. "And maybe give the cockatoo laryngitis."

"That too. Good thinking, *99*." I grinned. "Let's get ready first. I feel bad about calling her this early. I'll call her after six thirty." Ha, like that was much better, but she did tend to get up and go running around that time.

I went to the bathroom, washed my face, brushed my teeth, and put my hair in a low ponytail to accommodate the beanie that late autumn in Westerham demanded. By the time Liv and I made it downstairs, Mrs Soames and her bird were ensconced in the TV room, an early-morning news show blaring. I didn't think she was deaf—she certainly heard everything we said, although having Ethel screeching next to her ear had to have damaged something over the years.

When I texted Imani, she replied straight away. *See you in five.*

Be quiet when you get here. We still have "guests." I'll have to sneak you to the front door, and you can knock. That was the other thing about having a non-witch staying here—Angelica had to be super subtle when using magic, and I hadn't been able to practice either. Maybe I should ask Millicent if I could go there to practice and build up my strength. She was working from home now, as the baby was making things rather uncomfortable.

I shut the TV-room door with the excuse that I didn't want the TV to wake Angelica, which Mrs Soames thankfully was okay with, and waited outside the reception room. A quiet single tap sounded. I unlocked the door and opened it. Imani stood there, dressed in a jumper and jeans. I put my finger to my lips and led her to the front door. I opened it and quietly shut it so she could knock.

Knock, knock. I opened the door. "Imani! Imagine seeing you here so early." I laughed.

"I was thinking we could go for coffee and breakfast." She grinned.

"Sounds good to me. Come in, and I'll grab Liv." Before getting her, I poked my head into the TV room. "We're just going out, Mrs Soames. If you need anything, Angelica is upstairs."

"I'll be fine. I don't like to be a bother." She smiled sweetly. Grrr.

I didn't refute her claims, even though it galled me to stay quiet. "Bye."

As we walked to Costa in the drab, misty morning, Imani's breath plumed when she spoke. "How come she's still there?"

Olivia answered, "Her house is still haunted, and she has nowhere else to go. Her husband died a few years ago, and her only daughter moved to Australia."

"Can you blame her?" I asked. "Imagine living with Mrs Passive Aggressive. Oh, that's right, we don't have to imagine it."

Imani laughed. "Did her parrot wake you up again?"

Liv and I both nodded. "And she got me out of bed to show her where the tea was when she knew damned well it was in the cupboard above the kettle. The sooner she leaves, the better."

"Oh, don't be like that, Lily. She's an old duck. Surely she's not that bad."

I shook my head, and Liv said, "She is. Lily's not exaggerating this time."

Huh? "This time? When do I exaggerate?"

My friends smirked. I wasn't an embellisher. Sure, I was passionate about stuff sometimes, and maybe my enthusiasm came across as exaggeration, but I wasn't convinced. If anything, I tended to tone stuff down, not make a big deal out of things, especially if it was bad.

Imani sputtered a laugh. "We're just yanking your chain, love. Don't worry."

"You're not funny. You know that, right?"

We finally made it to Costa with no further insults, thank goodness. I wasn't in the mood. I hated being cranky, but I couldn't help it. I needed some good news, dammit. So much in my life lately had been negative: not being able to see Will, almost losing my magic, my new friend Jeremy going back to the States to work, and now our neighbour and her stupid cockatoo coming to stay. It was hard enough to deal with my life on ample sleep, but take that away, and you were creating a monster.

I pouted. "It doesn't open till seven. How did I not know this?" I checked my phone. Ten minutes to wait.

"You never get up early enough, and I didn't even notice the time," said Imani.

"What about you, Liv? You used to work here." I raised a brow.

She shrugged. "I didn't check what time it was when we left, and to be honest, I wanted to get you out of the house, and me too. Mrs Soames is a pain in the arse. You pointed out the tea to her three times yesterday, and I had to make her toast because she claimed she couldn't see the settings on the toaster. Then she left her dirty dishes for me to clean up."

"Maybe she thinks she's on holiday?" Imani snorted.

"If I was… better, I'd pop us over to Paris or something. A holiday sounds like a great idea." I tucked both hands under my arms. It was bloody freezing. "Why don't we keep walking down there. Five minutes there, five minutes back, and Costa will be open. It's too cold to stand around."

"You're so soft, Lily." Imani grinned. "Okay, let's go."

We headed down the hill, past the village green. "Oh, two of those terraces are for sale. They're quite cute." The two-storey narrow-fronted white buildings faced the green and were adorable with their dormer windows, if a bit small. They'd be perfect for someone wanting to live super close to everything. Whilst I'd love to buy my own place, I wasn't ready to sell my unit in Cronulla to fund a permanent relocation, and I didn't know if I could be comfortable in such a confined space, plus there wasn't any parking. It did make me think about living by myself though. Was I ready? Nah. Best to stay where I was for now. I had enough going on.

Three minutes down the road, we came across another

row of white terraces, their front doors opening directly onto the footpath. Each of the four terraces had a different coloured door—red, yellow, blue, then white. A Smith & Henderson real-estate sign proclaimed Sold. And next door, a grand two-storey orangey-brick home with large multi-paned, white-framed windows and imposing front door also had a Sold sign. We stopped walking, about to turn back, when I saw another For-Sale sign a few doors along as well.

"Can they redevelop this bit?" The suggestion sounded stupid, even as I said it—this was a historical area, and there was no way they'd knock down these places. It was just strange so many were for sale at the same time. I guess coincidence, or maybe the same person had owned it all, they'd died, and their family wanted to split up the proceeds?

"Definitely not." Olivia shook her head. "I guess the market must be good or something?"

"It's definitely a great time to be a real-estate agent." Imani laughed.

"Looks like it. But if there's a lot on the market, maybe the prices are dropping. Supply and demand." Hmm, they did photos and stuff for houses. Maybe I should try and get some of that work, add to my client base. "I'm going to call them later, see if they need a photographer, you know, for the advertising shots. If they're busy, maybe they're looking for someone?"

"Great idea, Lily." Liv smiled. No one said anything, but we were all thinking it: if I didn't get my magic back, there was little chance I'd be able to help the PIB with my photographic talent. I hadn't tried to see anything through the lens yet, though. Whenever I thought of it, my brain batted the idea away. Fear had the upper hand at the moment—contemplating never getting my talent back scared the crap out of me. Without my talent, we were less likely to find out what happened to my parents.

"Okay, Costa time!" I grinned and started the walk back up the hill. The cappuccino and double-chocolate muffin were likely to be the highlight of my day, so I planned to savour every bit of them.

WE RETURNED TO ANGELICA'S AT SEVEN FORTY-FIVE. OLIVIA and Imani both had work, although Imani made me promise that if I wanted to go anywhere, I'd text her. Angelica had given Imani office duties and a few witness interviews for a couple of cases they'd just solved, so she could be on call to babysit me if I went out. How demoralising. I was back to where I'd started when I'd first reached the UK—baby-witch status. Oh, how I wanted to scream.

I hurried up to my room in the interests of avoiding Mrs Soames and her pesky parrot. I briefly considered going back to bed—it looked so cosy and warm—but I was wide awake after my coffee and morning walk. Instead, I turned on my laptop and researched real-estate agents within a ten-mile radius. Ooh, there were a lot. I'd briefly done some real-estate photography back in Sydney for a company that sold advertising packages of copywriting, floor plan, and photos to selling agents. The work was easy, and I enjoyed stickybeaking through other people's houses.

Once 9:00 a.m. hit, I called the first company on my list —the one from the signs this morning— Smith & Henderson. I was expecting this to be hard work, so I almost fell off my chair when, after speaking to the director of residential sales of the Sevenoaks agency, he googled my website on the spot, checked out my work, and said to come for a trial job tomorrow. Woohoo! They had their usual photographer booked, and I'd be working for nothing so they could see how I did; then they'd let me know. He did say they'd been swamped lately and had even put on two extra agents a month ago. When I asked about their other local agencies, he suggested that if he liked my work, he'd liaise with the other agencies, as they'd been busy too. Right, well, I couldn't ask for more than that.

After ending the call, I grinned. I knew I was courting disaster by thinking maybe, just maybe, things were looking up. Well, could anyone blame me? Yeah, yeah, I should've known better, but I was an optimist, and I never went down without a fight.

CHAPTER 3

Day three of our delightful guests. My optimism was fading, and it was only six in the morning. After my Australianesque wake-up squawks, I'd gone down to find Mrs Soames rearranging the furniture in the lounge room. She'd moved the table between the Chesterfields, so it sat up against one wall, and she was attempting to coerce one of the three-seater lounges into a similar position. It wasn't having any of it, however, and stood in mute defiance of her rant that was replete with red face and waving fist. I stifled a snort. Couch: 1, Mrs Soames: 0.

Damn, she'd noticed me. "Well, what are you doing just standing there? Can't you see I need to move this silly lounge?"

Ethel sat on the windowsill and cawed, "Silly lounge,

rawrk! Silly lounge." More like silly Mrs Soames, but I wasn't going to go there.

"Um, why are you moving it?"

She rolled her eyes, then planted her hands on her hips. "I'm having the girls over for bridge later. Mayble's son and his friend are going to bring my dining table across and put it just there." She pointed to the space I assumed was going to be created between the Chesterfields and the armchairs at the other end of the room when she'd managed to move everything.

"Can't you just use the table in the kitchen?" She was complicating things that didn't need to be complicated. The more time I spent living with her, the more I realised that was her forte. Some people were talented at organisation, some cooking, some horse riding, and some, well, they were awesome at making everything harder. It was usually the people around them who suffered the most.

"It's not big enough."

Huh? "But it's the same size. They both seat six people, eight at a pinch."

She narrowed her eyes, and her head crept forward, zooming in on me. "Are you calling me a liar?"

Wow, that escalated quickly. "Ah, no." Okay, technically yes, but…. "I just think that maybe your estimating skills are out of whack." I was pretty pleased with how polite I'd managed to put it.

She stared at me, and I could practically see the little mouse wheels turning, trying to find a way to twist my words so she could have a go at me. She folded her arms, probably deciding she couldn't take this any further. "So, are you going to help me or not? It's not like I asked to be kicked out of my house by a ghost, you know." She sniffed, but the "poor me" effect was ruined by the crankily folded arms and sour expression on her face.

That was the million-dollar question, wasn't it? Hmm... I knew Angelica wouldn't care—it's not as if it was a permanent change, but something about pandering to Mrs Soames irked me. If I agreed to help with this, how far would she take it? Would she soon be moving all Angelica's stuff out and hers in? *Argh, all right, stupid conscience; I'll do it.* I resisted the urge to roll my eyes and moved to the Chesterfield. "Okay."

She smirked. Gah, the bitter taste of regret flooded my mouth. Note to self: next time, say no. As we finished moving the couches—well, when I'd finished moving them since she had the strength of a sparrow—a scratching noise tickled my ear. Oh my God! The cockatoo was sharpening its beak on Angelica's windowsill. "Ethel, stop that!"

The bird ignored me while Mrs Soames huffed indignantly. "How dare you speak to Ethel like that. Apologise!"

I stared at Mrs Soames, my face slack. *You have got to be kidding me.* "Please make your bird stop that, or I will. She's ruining the paint."

Her eyes snapped wide. "How dare you threaten my Ethel! If anything happens to her, I'm holding you accountable."

As if I'd hurt an animal. I was more thinking of getting the stupid bird back in its cage where it couldn't ruin anything except my sleep-ins. "I'm not going to hurt your cockatoo, Mrs Soames. Just make it stop ruining Angelica's house. I'm pretty sure she won't want you staying if you can't respect her house. It's not too much to ask."

She scowled at me and narrowed her eyes as much as she could without them actually closing. Then she huffed again and grabbed Ethel off the windowsill. She scratched her under the chin. "There, there, baby. It's okay. I won't let the bad lady hurt you."

What the actual hell? I gave up. This was too much for me to deal with BC—before coffee. I hurried to the kitchen, made my coffee, then took it up to my room. I wanted to check out Smith & Henderson real-estate ads to get a feel for the style they wanted. I'd found it was best not to reinvent the wheel when working for agencies. They all had their branding figured out, and anything that didn't fit inside that, no matter how awesome, was going to result in rejection.

After ascertaining they had a clean, simple style with natural lighting and little clutter in rooms, I shut my laptop and stared at the wall. It was only six thirty; my coffee was finished, and I had nothing to do. Stupid bird. How much longer were they staying? And had she done anything to banish the ghost? Surely there were priests who did that sort of thing. I opened my laptop again, typed "How do you banish a ghost" and hit Enter.

Who knew there were so many things you could do? To keep them out, you could put salt across your doors, and to get them to leave, you just had to ask firmly. I laughed.

Yeah, that hadn't worked. There was also smudging with a smudge stick, although, how that would force a ghost to leave, I didn't know. It might give a living person an asthma attack though. Ooh, Wiccans and Pagans could make a circle. Were Wiccans actual witches, or were they non-witches who thought they could make magical stuff happen? I'd have to ask Imani since she believed in ghosts. Angelica scoffed at our account but refused to go and see for herself. Typical.

The last resort, according to Summer Stream—cruel parents or was she a victim of her own making?—was to consult religious people who specialised in disruptive-spirit banishment. Ha, disruptive was one way to put it. Was that what happened to those kids in class who were always causing trouble? They grew up, died, and forever annoyed the hell out of other people. That would explain a lot.

I wrote down all the information, plus a small list of potential banishers—priests from local, and in two cases not so local, churches. Look at that; it was only quarter past seven. Argh. So long to wait until I could leave to go to my appointment. With nothing left to do, I grabbed my iPad and read. Okay, so maybe having nothing to do wasn't such a bad thing.

Finally it was time to pack and go. I'd called Imani last night, and she was going to quietly tail me—it would look weird if I turned up with a bodyguard or an assistant. As far as I was concerned, she didn't exist, and I probably wouldn't see her if she was doing her job properly. That made me kind of sad because I liked Imani, but when she was on duty, she didn't want distractions, and we didn't need the snake group knowing I had protection. Maybe they'd show themselves if they thought I was by myself. Being a decoy was not my favourite thing to do, but I was almost used to it. Living in fear had become second nature. Maybe that's why I'd been crabby lately—the constant stress, which I thought I could ignore. It seemed everything caught up with you eventually. Poop.

I grabbed all my equipment and changed into my standard photographer outfit: black jeans, shirt, and boots, plus a black winter coat. I crept downstairs, to avoid Mrs Soames hearing me—I did not want to get into another conversation with her. The TV was blaring, so it was an easy no-notice exit, and I hadn't even needed a spell.

It was a picturesque three–four-minute drive to Brasted, a village just to the east of Westerham. Farmland filled most of the distance between locales, with pretty Tudor terraces and early 1900s brick homes lining the main road into the village centre. I turned left, off the main road, and followed the road up a small hill. The home was part way along, on a block that sloped to the side, framed by a white picket fence. Cute.

I parked across the street from the two-storey sandstone house, took out my gear, and walked over to knock on the front door. My palms were sweating—damn nerves. What if the agent hated me? What if they were really difficult? Argh. *Stop thinking.* I finally worked up the courage to knock.

The agent opened the door. Dressed in a navy-blue suit, white shirt, and dark tie, his grey hair cut neatly but not too short, he was rather distinguished. His accent matched the look—refined in a very English way. Maybe distinguished should be changed to distenglished. I clamped my teeth together to stop my nervous laughter. Bad time to make a joke with myself.

I placed my gear on the small, uncovered tiled area that acted as the porch so I could shake his proffered hand. "Welcome to Brasted, Lily. I'm Oliver Smith, owner of the Sevenoaks office. Lovely to meet you." He smiled, his greeting genuine and not at all salesy, but then, I wasn't here to buy anything.

"Lovely to meet you too, Mr Smith. Thanks for giving me a chance to show you my work."

"Call me Oliver, please. Our other photographer is setting up in the back garden, so if you want to get some front shots, that would be good. Then we want all the normal internals: bedrooms, sitting room, dining, kitchen, bathroom. If you can get a few of each so we can pick the best ones later. I'll have you do your back-garden photos when you're done."

"Sounds good. And is it okay for me to move stuff out of the picture if it's cluttering things, like from tables and kitchen benchtops?"

"Ordinarily, yes, but we've had this house styled, and the owners have already moved out, so it's always tidy. We've kept the clutter to a minimum, and we want to keep the recipe book that's on the kitchen bench."

"Okay, great. Why don't I get started?"

"If you have any questions, let me know. I'll just shut

this door, and when you want to come in, just come on through, but take off your shoes—they've just had the carpet cleaned."

He left me to do my thing, which was awesome. I hated working with people looking over my shoulder, especially if I didn't know them. It was nerve-wracking enough doing a job for a new client without being judged from close quarters the whole time. I set up my tripod and took photos from two different positions—one slightly down the hill looking up, and one straight in front. When I was done, I took my boots off and went inside.

I looked through each room before I went back and set up to photograph them. At least the agent and current photographer knew their stuff: all curtains and blinds were open, and the lights were mostly off. I had my extra flash to bounce off the ceiling if I needed more light. Because I didn't know this client, I took shots with and without flash in each room. I gathered my boots from the front door and carried them through the house to the back so I could finish up with the yard and back-of-the-house shots.

After I'd photographed the backyard, the agent met me outside. "Mind if I have a look at what you've done?"

I smiled and ignored the way my heart sped up. I set my camera up so he could scroll through the photos. "Here you go."

After looking through about half of them, he said, "These are great, Lily." He kept scrolling in silence.

The lack of conversation gave me hives. I didn't know where to look—if I looked at him to gauge for a reaction, which I couldn't help doing, it would be creepy, and if I wandered around looking at random stuff in the yard, it would also be strange. So I did what any awkward Lily did: I made inane conversation. "How's the market going? I noticed you guys have a lot for sale around Westerham."

He handed the camera back, but his pleasant expression had turned guarded. "The market is generally stable, but around here, it's dropped in the last month or two. Supply and demand. We've had a lot more stock than usual."

"Oh, why is that?" I wasn't sure if I really cared or if I was still talking for the heck of it.

"Are you in the market to buy?"

"Ah, no. I live with my aunt, and she's got a big place." A little white lie wouldn't hurt, and Angelica was practically an aunt to me.

"She's not looking to sell in the near future?" He cocked his head to the side as if encouraging me to say yes. Weird. I mean, why would he need to encourage more sales if they had too many properties as it was? Although, they probably didn't care what price the owners sold for—as long as they agreed to sell to someone, the agent would get their commission.

"Um, not that I know of. She's been there for a long time."

He handed me his card. "If she changes her mind, just give me a call." His smile was carefully constructed to be pleasant yet not desperate, or maybe that was his normal smile, and I was reading too much into things. "You'd be surprised how quickly things can change."

I drew my brows down. What was that supposed to mean? Should I ask? No, that would seem rude, or would it?

"Hey, Oliver, I'm done. See you at the next one." The other photographer, a short, slim guy about my age was half in, half out of the French doors to the garden.

"See you there, Rob." Oliver turned to me. "I like your work, Lily. Edit those shots and send them all to the email I sent earlier—it's not the same as what's on my card. We like to keep all advertising-related emails in the one spot, or things can get missed."

"Of course. I'll do that tonight."

"Great. We do have a twenty-four-hour turnaround time on all photographs, so best to get on board with that from the get-go. And thanks for coming out."

"Thanks for giving me a trial." I bent to undo the zipper on my boots in preparation of walking back through the house.

"Oh, don't worry about that. You can use the side gate." Well, that was easier. Lugging my boots, tripod, and camera bag would have been a struggle.

I picked up my things and let myself out. There was no sign of Imani up or down the street. Maybe she had a no-notice spell on the car, and my lack of powers meant I was virtually a non-witch? I sighed and pouted. I never thought I'd be in a position to want my powers back. But here I was.

Two things I was grateful for today: a plate of freshly baked scones with jam and cream was in the fridge waiting for me for afternoon tea, and the job had been easy. The agent had been pleasant enough, but things did get weird at the end. What did he mean by "things can change"? My unsettled stomach grumbled all the way home, and it wasn't because it was hungry. "What are you trying to tell me?" It gurgled a couple of times. "Is a boy stuck down the well? Is his leg broken?" I snorted. Being stupid was better than stressing the whole way home. It was just a shame that my stomach couldn't articulate actual words; then I'd never be lonely.

When I got home, I turned into our driveway... and slammed my foot on the brake. The seat belt dug into my chest as I jerked forward. "Ow! What the hell?" Four cars took up all the space. Four cars I'd never seen before. Had something happened? Adrenaline shot through me, unsettling my stomach even more. Until I remembered Mrs Soames and Ethel were having a bridge party. I rolled my eyes—boy, were they getting a workout. Would her friends be as hostile as she was? Had they all brought their pets? The universe wouldn't be so cruel... would it?

I was about to find out.

CHAPTER 4

I walked in the door to classical music and the loud chatter of a tableful of old ladies playing cards. I was quiet and only stuck my head in quickly. No one noticed, well, except for Ethel, who was back on her perch on Angelica's damaged windowsill. She spread her wings and screeched, "Intruder, intruder!" Stupid bird. I managed to flee up the stairs before anyone saw me, but I'd had time enough to see they were using Angelica's best china tea set. It had been handed down from her mother. She was not going to be happy.

Safely in my room, I edited the photos for the morning, my stomach tense, waiting for Mrs Soames to knock on my door and ask for a four-course lunch. Thankfully, lunchtime came and went without incident. I considered calling Angelica, but all the bad news could wait till she got home, and who knew—by then, I'd probably have more to tell her. Might as well do it all at once.

By two thirty, I'd pressed Send on the real-estate stuff, and I was starving. *Scones with jam and cream* repeated in my head. Mmm. This time when my stomach growled, it was all about the food. Clearly, the trip outside my room couldn't be put off any longer.

Fingers crossed, I slowly opened the door. I held my breath and listened. Classical music and the murmur of voices floated up the stairs. Yep, her friends were still here. What time would they leave? Maybe it was a good thing, as Mrs Soames would be too busy to listen for me. I took a deep, fortifying breath and stepped out to commence Operation Eat All the Scones.

I slowly crept downstairs, avoiding the creaky tread. I'd have to be quick near the bottom of the stairs, as I'd be visible from the lounge room. Although only someone sitting at end of the table would be able to see me, it was still risky. Oh, how I wished for my magic back in its entirety. Straining for an hour to do something as simple as light a flame depressed me—it used the least amount of energy. God knew when I would be able to do anything meaningful again. I swallowed my forlorn sigh, just in case any of the oldies had supersonic hearing.

Okay, this was it. Time to run. I quietly sped down the remaining stairs and flew past the door—silent running was harder than it sounded. I made it to the kitchen and headed straight for the fridge. A spurt of saliva drenched my mouth at my proximity to the scones, jam, and cream.

There was only a fridge door separating us. I grinned as I opened it.

Middle shelf: not there. Top shelf: not there. Bottom shelf: nope. I scrunched my forehead. Maybe someone had put them in the vegetable drawer, which would be weird but not impossible. I slid it open. Tomatoes, celery, and carrots, but no scones. I frowned, shut the fridge, and turned to survey every bench. Nothing. Where the hell had my scones gone?

"There you are, Lily. Elizabeth said she saw someone dash past, so I thought I'd check and make sure it was a person and not a ghost." Gah, busted.

"Ah, yeah. I was just coming down to grab something to eat."

"I'd offer you some of our refreshments, but they're all gone. Beatrice brought the most delicious tea cake, and I found some scones in the fridge, which was fortuitous—it saved me a trip to the shops." She smiled. Was there satisfaction in that grin, or was I just imagining it?

I gnashed my back teeth together as anger sizzled from my toes up through my stomach to my fists, which I clenched until they ached. She. Ate. My. Scones. My stomach growled.

Mrs Soames turned and walked away while I stood rigid and shaking, my insides almost on fire. *I want my scones back.*

She'd pushed me too far.

The heat inside me shot through my arms and hands, dissipating and leaving my skull tingling. Retching came from the lounge room, and someone screamed. What the hell? My eyes were wide, and I slapped my hand over my mouth. Had I accidentally cast a spell?

I trotted to the lounge room and bit my bottom lip— what was I about to find? The retching stopped just as I walked through the door. *Oh, God, the smell.* I gagged.

Mrs Soames and three of her friends sat in their chairs in varying states of disgusted surprise. Vomit coated the table in front of the four women, and two of them were wiping their mouths with the backs of their sleeves. One of them, her purple perm still perky and oblivious, seemed to be frozen with her eyes wide and mouth open. Actually, she wasn't frozen—she blinked intermittently, like a light bulb that couldn't decide if it was going to live or die.

The two friends who had no vomit on or around their person slowly backed away from the disaster. Maybe this would encourage them all to go home. But why had they vomited?

Mrs Soames had recovered somewhat and stared at her friend. "What was in that cake, Beatrice? This is all your fault!"

The one who must be Beatrice was one of the women who were discreetly trying to leave. She stopped and her mouth dropped open. "How dare you accuse me! I ate it too, and I'm not sick. But you know what I didn't eat?" She lifted her chin and paused for what must be dramatic impact. "Those scones that *you* put on the table." Oh, crap. I lifted my fingers and covered my mouth. Had I accidentally cast a spell? There was the heat in my stomach, the tingling scalp. I cringed. Oops. On the bright side, I might have my magic back, or at least almost at full strength, and I had Mrs Soames to thank… and the scones that were, um, ew.

Everyone turned accusing glares to Mrs Soames. More than one of the old ladies had their lips pressed together. Beatrice folded her cardigan-clad arms. "Well? What have you got to say for yourself, Mrs High and Mighty?"

"Get out, and don't bother coming back until you can be polite to your host." Mrs Soames stood, and some of the half-digested food fell from her lap to the floor with a little splat sound. I gagged again. "I said, get out of my house!" *Her house?* We so needed to get rid of her before she kicked us out too.

"Get out, rawrk! Get out!" The bird bounced up and down, really getting into the drama. It was kind of funny and reminded me of those Facebook videos of dancing cockatoos. I bit my tongue to stop the giggle threatening to emerge.

"You heard Ethel. I want you all gone before I come back." Mrs Soames looked at the windowsill. "Come on, Ethel." Then she spun quickly, too quickly for a woman of her advanced years, and wobbled. I instinctively jerked my arms forward and moved towards her in case I needed to execute a catch. She oscillated but then righted herself and stormed out— Ethel flapping in her wake—leaving her card-playing companions gaping after her.

Once she was gone, one of the vomit-covered ladies started crying. The woman looked down at her soiled clothes in despair. Gah, it wasn't her fault any of this had happened—it was Mrs Soames's fault and mine. I pinched my nose and breathed through my mouth. "Would you like to have a shower? I can lend you some clothes. My aunt is only a little taller than you and about the same build. She won't mind."

The lady looked up at me, eyes red. The poor thing. "I'd appreciate that. Thank you." She stood.

"Okay, then. Why don't we get you cleaned up." I addressed the other two women who had fallen victim to my temper. "The offer is there for both of you too." One of the ladies was rather fatter than Angelica, but maybe I could call Angelica and get her to magic me some bigger clothes. Even though I'd made people vomit, I didn't know how much of my magic had returned and if it was going to be consistent. Maybe it would come back in stages?

The larger lady, who had vomited more on the table than on herself shook her head. "Thank you for the offer, but I live two minutes away. I'm going home." She stood, grabbed her bag, and left.

The other one, who was the smallest of them and sparrow-like with delicate bone structure, nervous movements, and dyed-brown hair—I figured because what eighty-year-old had brown hair—said in a soft voice to one of her friends, "Do you mind me coming with you now? I just want to go home." As she put her hands on the table and pushed her chair back, it was clear her hands were trembling.

"I'm so sorry about this."

One of the healthy ladies turned to me. "It's not your fault. If it's anyone's fault, it's Mary's. That's the last time I play cards with her." She turned to the sparrow lady. "Of course I'll take you home, Sonia. Let's go."

After they all filed out, I gathered Angelica's clothes and a towel and showed the last woman to the bathroom. When she was done and gone, I returned to the scene of the crime. Argh, what a mess. I sighed. Time to clean up, and I couldn't use my magic because, provided I was capable, Mrs Stupid Soames could come in at any moment. She was really cramping my style. Okay, so it was more than that. She was driving me crazy, eating my scones, moving her furniture in, and waking me up early. That wasn't even the worst part. Having to fear walking through your own home because you might come across a mean, cranky person was stressful. It was worse than walking on eggshells—it was more like walking on thumbtacks.

My gag reflex got a massive workout while cleaning the disaster. When I was done, I had a shower because even after washing my hands, the acrid smell was still there. Stubborn little spew particles.

Around four thirty, my phone rang. "Hello, Lily speaking."

"Hi, Lily, it's Oliver Smith, the agent from this morning."

Yikes. Was this going to be good news or bad? And as if I'd forgotten him from this morning, although a lot had happened. "Hi, Oliver. Did you get the photos?"

"I did, thank you. You've done an outstanding job, and I'm calling to offer you some paid work. I have two jobs for tomorrow. Are you able to attend?"

I grinned and fist-pumped the air. *Woohoo!* "I would love to. Thanks!"

"Great. I'll email you the details. The first job's at nine, and the second one is at ten thirty. They're about five minutes from each other."

"Okay. I'll see you tomorrow at nine."

"Wonderful. And welcome aboard. I'll also email you our standard contractor agreement. If you could also bring a signed copy with you when you come, that would be helpful."

"Will do. And thanks again. Bye!"

"Bye, Lily."

And that was that. Yay! Getting another client felt like a milestone. Despite all the setbacks, I was slowly building a life and career here, and it was always exciting when someone liked my work, even if it was just for real-estate advertising. And let's not forget it was something to get me out of the house and away from Mrs Stupid Soames. Win, win, win. I grinned again and texted Olivia my great news. Then I called Imani.

"Hi, love. What's up?"

"I've got some more real-estate photography work for tomorrow morning. Are you okay to come with?"

"Of course. What time?"

"I'm not sure, but my first job is at nine. I can't see it being too far away, but I'll text you when I get the email. I'd say I'll leave around eight forty-five, but I'll confirm. I should need you until about eleven."

"Consider it done. I'll see you tomorrow."

"Thanks. Bye!" Well, the day had ended on a high note, although compared to what had happened with Mrs Soames and the scones, just about anything would be considered a high note. I was tempted to practice some magic in my room, but if this afternoon was a fluke, I didn't want to know that now when I was on a roll. Okay, so one good thing wasn't a roll, but I took what I could get.

At six thirty, there was a knock on my door. *Please don't be Mrs Soames.* Could I pretend I wasn't here? I eyed the wardrobe. I could definitely fit.

"Lily, are you in there?"

Phew, it was Angelica. "Yes. Come in."

She came in, shut the door behind her, and mumbled something. Goosebumps whispered across my scalp. "A silence spell, but for anyone eavesdropping the normal way."

"Ah, okay. And I felt it." I grinned. Looks like this afternoon hadn't been a fluke.

Angelica smiled. "That's wonderful, Lily." Her smile disappeared. "Would you like to tell me what happened here today?" Trust her to dispense with the happy stuff as soon as possible. Couldn't I roll in the joy of getting my magic back a little longer?

I started with Mrs Soames having her table brought in and finished with the last lady leaving. "I know she has nowhere to go, but we can't live with her forever. What are we going to do?"

"I'm going to start by going to her house tonight. You know I don't believe in ghosts, but I'm willing to concede I could be wrong. But if it's not a ghost, there has to be a logical reason for the manifestation. Either way, we do need to deal with it."

Finally. Why couldn't she have done this on the first night? No one ever listened to my advice until everyone was at breaking point. Maybe I was cursed or something? Kind of the reverse of the boy who cried wolf—the girl who just cried. Yep, that was me.

I didn't really want to ask the next question, but I couldn't resist. As much as I tried not to think about it, I missed him so much my heart hurt. The sadness had been on my back since we'd "broken up." Its arms held tight around my neck, relentlessly suffocating. I didn't know how to dislodge it—the longer we'd had no contact, the harder it was. "Have you heard from Will?"

A shadow darkened her features, then was gone as her poker face slid into place. She shook her head but said nothing.

"Is his assignment particularly dangerous, or is it… you know?" My heart kicked up a few dozen notches. Will was on an undercover assignment, but he was deep undercover for his *other* assignment, which was to infiltrate Dana's snake group. I was betting it was the Dana assignment that was worse.

Angelica waggled her fingers, and my scalp tingled again. "Okay, we have a traditional bubble of silence too. Lily, we haven't heard from Will. He didn't check in yesterday when he was supposed to, and his mission for the PIB isn't so dangerous that he couldn't have checked in."

Her face gave nothing away, but her body was rigid, back too straight, face too set—the effort of showing no emotion was obviously difficult.

That just left the other option—Regula Pythonissam— Dana's crew. Had they killed him? My stomach dropped into a chasm, taking my blood with it. My head spun. If I hadn't been sitting down, I would have ended up on the floor. This couldn't be happening.

"I'm sorry to say it is, Lily." Damn lack of mind-shield. Now that I had some power back, I'd have to get into the habit of putting it in place every morning. "I've put two of my best and most trustworthy agents on it. I managed to keep your brother and Beren out of this. If they've… if they've killed William, there's nothing they won't do, which puts anyone close to you in extreme danger."

"Can we have another meeting? We need to move quicker on this. It's not just about my parents. None of us are safe until we stop them. And Will…." My heart constricted, and for a moment, I couldn't breathe.

"I know, Lily, but we can't rush in. They may not have hurt him at all. The alternative is that he's fostering Dana's trust, and he can't risk checking in."

I shook my head. "That doesn't make sense. She would know he has to check in for his other assignment. Surely he would've told her that. And he knows not contacting you would ring alarm bells." Dread drew its blade tip down my back, sharp and cold. I shivered, and the hairs on my nape jumped to attention. "We have to do something."

It was her turn to shake her head. "It could be a trap.

Maybe he's doing well, fooling them all, and she's dared him not to contact us to see if we come rushing in to save him. We usually wait five days to go after an agent who's on assignment. We have to follow protocol, as much as I don't like it. I'm sorry, Lily, but we're following procedure on this one."

I clenched my fists and bit my tongue to banish the tears that burned my eyes. Tears wouldn't sway Angelica, and I refused to cry until I knew there was something to cry about. I'd know if Will were... dead, wouldn't I? I was a witch, and we had a strong bond, so surely I'd have felt something. Or maybe I was overly romantic, and being that deeply connected to someone was a fallacy. I took a deep breath. "Okay."

"I know it's hard, Lily. Truly I do." Her eyes held sadness, bone-weary and worn in. What secrets did she keep? Who had she lost along the way?

I jumped up and threw my arms around her. Neither of us were super affectionate, but it was clear we both needed a hug. Her arms slid around me, and we stood that way for a minute before she stepped back, a gentle, resigned smile on her face. "We do what we must, Lily. The truth is that life is rarely easy for anyone. Everyone makes sacrifices at some point, and unfortunately, being associated with the PIB means that maybe the sacrifice you make is the person you love the most."

Was she talking about Will sacrificing our relationship, or me having to sacrifice him to find my parents? Either way was depressing. Until I knew the truth, I'd assume he was alive. There was no way I'd be able to function otherwise. Time to change the subject. "Can we go look for the ghost now?" I didn't want to see it again, but I wanted to make sure Angelica did.

"Okay, dear. I'll grab the key from Mrs Soames, and we'll go."

I donned my thick coat and boots—even though it was just across the road, she hadn't been home, so the heating hadn't been on, and this little Aussie still hadn't acclimatised. Oh, and ghosts made things colder. The things I had to prepare for. Sheesh.

The rising moon haloed the clouds in shining silver. Its clean light shone through the gaps and created shadows on the ground. Angelica strode confidently to the house while I scurried behind her, every nerve poised to fire at the slightest provocation. She slid the key into the lock and turned, shoving the door open in her no-nonsense way. Even if she saw the ghost, she probably wouldn't be rattled. That didn't make me feel any better though—bravery wasn't always a great survival tactic. Just ask the idiots who think they can pat a lion in a wildlife reserve. Oh, that's right, we can't; they're dead.

I hung back as she walked into the hall. Halfway down, she turned and raised a brow at me. "Are you coming in?"

Fear left a metallic tang in my mouth, but if anything happened to Angelica, and I could've helped, I'd never forgive myself. Fighting my better judgement, I stepped inside. The floorboard creaked, and I started. Damn my racing heart. Angelica shook her head, a smirk playing on her face. *Yes, well, have your smirk. I'll have mine later when the ghost attacks.*

"Come on. Let's get this over with. I have a report to finish." She flicked the light on in the living room and entered. I followed, constantly looking over my shoulder. That ghost could come from anywhere.

Angelica looked at the nearly empty side of the room. "Is that where her dining table was?"

"Yes. Are you going to make her put it back th—"

The temperature plummeted from about ten degrees to what felt like zero. Crap. I shared a look with Angelica and shivered. A voice boomed from behind me. "Get out! I told you to get out! This is my domain."

I spun around. The ugly ghost hovered in front of the hallway door. His teeth were bared, as was his fat, hairy torso. Why couldn't ghosts be buff young men? You'd probably welcome one of those in your house. It wouldn't be like being haunted at all. But life didn't work like that. Of course not. Not that I wished any young man dead. *Hmm, maybe I should rethink all that.*

"Why don't you make us?"

What the hell? I jerked my head around. Angelica's feet were planted hip-width apart, and her hands were firmly on her hips. My eyes widened. "What are you doing? You'll provoke it."

She rolled her eyes. "Look, ghost, it's time for you to leave. Mrs Soames has nowhere to go, and she can't stay with us much longer. Now go!"

The ghost's brows drew down. Anger radiated from it in

waves. Where was Mrs Soames's back door? I needed to get out of there. "I will never leave. Never!" A door slammed somewhere else in the house. I jumped.

I split my frantic gaze between Angelica and the ghost. "Ah, I think we should go. It's obvious he doesn't want to go anywhere, so why don't we?" That was the logical conclusion as far as I could tell, plus I didn't know how much longer I could hold off wetting myself. Being scared to death was hard work.

"Why this house, hmm? Mrs Soames has lived here for years, and you show up all of a sudden. You should go back to where you came from."

"Never! Anyone who lives here will face my wrath and die. Stay at your own peril." It darted around the room, passing two paintings, knocking each one off the wall. They landed with a crash of broken glass. The shards lifted off the floor. Oh, crap. I didn't have much magic to defend myself with, and what if magic was no protection against a supernatural being? Angelica could be about to cop a shredding.

"Come here, Lily." I hurried to her, wondering why I was running the opposite way to where I actually wanted to go, which was the hallway. She mumbled something, and a protective shield formed around us. It shimmered as it oscillated. Through it, I looked longingly at the opening to the hallway and freedom. "Don't worry. Nothing can touch us in here."

"Prepare to die!" the apparition screamed. The deadly projectiles launched. My eyes shut tight, and I dropped to the floor in a crouch, my arms protecting my face. I trusted Angelica, but not that much. She'd never been in a situation like this as far as I knew, so her assumptions could be wrong.

Hmm, Angelica wasn't screaming. The sound of glass smashing filled the room. I opened my eyes. A carpet of twinkling fragments littered the floor in front of the shield. "See, I told you." Angelica smiled. Well, someone was self-righteous today.

"There's no need to be smug. Admit it; you didn't know it would work."

"Didn't I?"

That was such a non-answer and, I was betting, an admission of guilt. I was willing to let it go since it had saved our lives. Getting out when I said to also would have saved our lives. But no one ever listened to me…. "Are we going to get out of here now? Please?"

She pressed her lips together, considering.

"Leave now, or suffer the consequences." His voice rumbled over us, vibrating uncomfortably through my bones. I looked up at Angelica—yes, I was still on the floor —my eyes imploring her. *Please say we can go.*

She stared at the ghost, then back at me. "All right. We can go." Yes, for mind reading!

"Yay!" I jumped up.

"I'll drop the shield on three. Then we run. I'll come after you, okay?"

"Can't we just run with it around us?"

"It won't move. If you want a strong shield, it has to be stuck in place. One, two, three!"

The shimmering vanished, and I sprinted all the way to the street without looking back. I checked to make sure Angelica was right behind me before I made a cursory glance for cars—I didn't need to add getting run over to my list of problems. Then I raced across the road and into our house. I never wanted to go through that again.

Funny how the universe never respected what I wanted. When was I going to stop wishing for the impossible?

CHAPTER 5

After we'd gotten home, Angelica refused to talk about what happened and insisted she had some thinking to do before we deliberated on a solution. Olivia was at her parents' for dinner, so after Angelica, our guest, and I had eaten, I hotfooted it to bed. I wanted no more dramas, and I knew that the stupid cockatoo would be waking me up at the crack of dawn. Not getting enough sleep had made me cranky, and I wanted to be at my best for my first two proper real-estate jobs tomorrow.

After a thankfully decent night of sleep, I managed to make it to the first job on time. And now, at my last job, I stood in one corner of the library in a six-bedroom, two-storey c. 1880s home, my camera sitting atop my tripod. A timber fireplace was at one end of the room, and dark timber shelves lined the three other walls. A blue Persian rug sat in the centre of the space, which was filled with armchairs and smoking tables. A stuffed ostrich sat in one corner, and a taxidermied deer head surveyed the room from above the mantlepiece. Library: good. Taxidermied head: not good. And what was with the ostrich? Maybe they got their decorating style from *Hunting* magazine. I didn't actually know if there was such a magazine, but I would bet there was.

As I set up my flash—the room was rather dark, even with the two windows—the owner came in. Oliver had said owners weren't often at the property when we did the advertising stuff, and in Australia they rarely were, but today was going to be different, apparently. The woman must have been in her mid-thirties and was slim, taller than me by a couple of inches, and had long, brown hair that had been styled in soft curls. She was fully made-up, including false eyelashes. Why did women bother? I couldn't imagine how much time it wasted each day. It would take me an hour to do all that, and then there was the undoing before bed. I seriously needed to get to work on the "I think I look fantastic" spell.

Mrs Jennings—the agent had introduced us earlier—came over to me. Her smile seemed unsure. Maybe she was worried about my skills. People often thought I was younger than twenty-four, and I guessed they didn't trust I knew what I was doing. "How are the photos going?"

"Really well. After I'm done here, I'll be getting some shots of the back garden."

"Hopefully the rain will hold off." She gazed outside.

"It should be fine, and if not, I can still get out there. I've got protective plastic for my gear." There was no need to tell her I'd needed it for my PIB work. She was a non-witch, and I didn't want to lose my job on the first day. Not that the witch laws left me any room to divulge either.

She gazed at me for a few seconds while I adjusted the flash to the right angle. It was as if she wanted to ask me something but didn't know how. Well, if the question was super important, she'd get to it, or not. I just had to keep on with the job I was here to do, so I checked the settings on my camera and clicked off a test shot. Slightly dark. I slowed the shutter speed and put the next shot on delayed timer. I pressed the button and counted to five. The shot clicked. Much better.

"Ah, Lily, isn't it?"

"Yes, Mrs Jennings." I straightened and looked at her with a gentle smile—I didn't want to startle her. She was a lot like the deer watching from the wall. "Did you want to ask me something?"

"Um, yes, as a matter of fact. Have you seen anything… unusual in your photos, or are they all good?"

"Unusual?" Had they painted over massive settlement cracks in the brickwork or something?

"So there's nothing in your photos that shouldn't be there?"

"I'm not really sure what you mean, but here, you can have a look for yourself." I stepped aside so she could flick through the shots I'd taken.

She bit her bottom lip as she scrolled through. When she

was done, her shoulders relaxed and lowered. What had been bothering her? "I've been a photographer for a few years. I'll make sure your home looks as gorgeous in the photos as it is in real life." Because it was a perfectly presented property, full of character and high-end finishes, despite the dead-animal head, which some people actually liked. Couldn't say I related, but to each their own. Maybe she was worried because she was a perfectionist?

She blinked. "Oh, no. Sorry, Lily. It's not like that at all. I trust Oliver to produce a good campaign, although if it's as my neighbour said, it won't be on the market for long. Oliver has a great list of buyers ready and waiting. Which is a relief, really."

"Oh, have you already bought somewhere else?"

"Ah, no. This was a spur-of-the-moment thing, but we need to get out quickly."

"Hello, ladies." Oliver strode into the room. "How are you going, Lily?"

"Hi. I just have to finish this room, then the back of the property, and that's it."

"Oh good. Just a reminder, I need to be gone in ten minutes, and Lisa has to get to work."

Lisa—or Mrs Jennings, as I was supposed to call her—gave a nervous laugh. "Of course, yes."

"Where do you work?" I couldn't help being friendly, even if I was wasting time and I was supposed to be impressing my new client. The ten minutes was ticking down, apparently.

"At Tunbridge Wells Museum. I had the morning off for this, but I have to be back by twelve."

"I won't be much longer."

Oliver accompanied Mrs Jennings out while I took the photos I needed and hurried to the backyard. Once I was done there, I said goodbye and left. The whole thing had left me... concerned. Hmm, maybe that wasn't the right word, but Mrs Jennings had given off a weird vibe, and Oliver might have been in a hurry, but it was as if he was trying to stop us from chatting. But why?

On the five-minute drive home, my phone rang. My heart skipped a beat at the chance it might be Will. I pulled over and looked at the screen. Nope. My breaths pushed through the sadness as my heart reluctantly kept on beating. It was Oliver. "Hello, Lily speaking."

"Hi, Lily, it's Oliver."

"Oh, hi. Did I forget something?" Yikes. I hope I hadn't stuffed up on the first day.

"Nothing like that. I just wanted to ask you not to chat to the homeowners on the job. We're usually on a tight schedule, and we don't want the owners thinking they can tell us how to run the advertising campaign. It happens more often than you'd think. If one of them talks to you, just be polite, but don't be chatty. Understood?"

Oh crap. I was in trouble. I sighed quietly. "Ah, yes, of course. I'll make sure I keep it to a hello and goodbye."

"Great to hear. I knew I could count on you. Thanks again for today. I can't wait to see them in my inbox tonight.

There's more work coming your way. Have a wonderful day."

"Thanks, Oliver. You too. Bye."

"Bye."

There went any confusion over whether he was trying to stop the conversation or not. But why? His reasons sounded lame. It was easy to pander to someone. Smile at the client, nod, agree, but then do what you were paid to do—provide quality photos that would help sell the house. And Mrs Jennings hadn't tried to tell me where to stand. She didn't even criticise any of the pictures I'd already taken. So what was really going on?

I pondered that question while I edited the photos. I took extra care with Mrs Jennings's, but I couldn't see anything unusual. What had she meant by weird? I guess I'd never know. How irritating.

When I finished, I emailed them all to Oliver and went on their website to check out the other properties they had for sale. Huh, was that normal? There were pages of properties, but they were all sold. Every. Single. One. That wasn't normal, was it? Especially here, where there could be a chain of buyers and sellers linked together where nothing could happen until the original lot settled. It was a crazy system, as far as I was concerned, because it meant you could be waiting to close on your new home for months.

I visited one of their London-office websites. Some properties were sold, but most were for sale. That confirmed this was unusual. So what the hell was going on? I also googled house prices in Kent. A couple of articles came up, saying that property prices had fallen for the past three months, but only in Kent. The rest of the UK was stable, maybe down a percentage or two. Kent prices, on average, had fallen up to 15 percent. Ouch.

This was getting stranger and stranger, and I was going to find out why.

※

THE SWEET AROMA OF GARLIC WAFTED AROUND THE kitchen. I'd cooked spaghetti bolognaise the normal way since Angelica couldn't magic dinner into existence. It smelled so good, and my stomach grumbled. I placed the huge bowl in the middle of the table and called out, "It's ready. Come and get it," then sat in my seat. My mouth watered as I waited for everyone. If only it wasn't rude to serve myself and start eating.

Angelica came in, followed by Mrs Soames. They both sat opposite me, Mrs Soames eyeing the bowl of spaghetti and wrinkling her nose. "Garlic upsets my stomach."

"I'm sorry, but I didn't know." Was it wrong of me to be happy about that? She'd given us all much more than a stomach ache since she'd been here. It was only fair that I repaid the favour. I knew it was mean, but sometimes I was a substandard human. I was working on being perfect, but I had a long way to go.

"If you would rather, there's bread and sandwich ingredients in the fridge." Angelica picked up the serving tongs and looked at Mrs Soames. "Or would you like some of the spaghetti?" I bit back a smirk. I loved it when she was on my side.

Mrs Soames had done as little as she could while she'd been here, and I knew her answer before she said, "Well, I suppose I could try the dinner. I'll just have to take an antacid later."

Olivia walked in with mail in her hand. "I'm not late, am I?"

I smiled. "Just in time. I've set you a place." I nodded at the bowl next to mine.

"Thanks, Lily. Ooh, my favourite!" She grinned, then looked at Mrs Soames. "Here's your mail." She handed it to her, put our mail on the kitchen countertop, and sat next to me.

"How was your day?" I asked her.

"Busy." She heaped spaghetti into her plate and passed me the tongs. Because of Mrs Soames, there was no elaborating on why or how she'd been busy.

I filled my plate and sprinkled some parmesan on the top. Angelica swallowed. "This is really good, Lily. Thanks for cooking."

I smiled. "My pleasure. Glad you like it."

Mrs Soames ate a couple of mouthfuls and placed her fork down to peruse her mail. She checked the two letters and grabbed a folded piece of paper with no envelope. "Oh, this is from Smith & Henderson. What do they want? Nuisance real-estate agents." She put her glasses on and read the letter. When she finished, she folded it up, put it back on the table, and resumed eating. Liv and I exchanged eye-rolls. Typical of Mrs Soames to goad us into asking. If there was any way to be difficult and annoying, she'd find it. What a talent.

"Have you thought about when you're going home, Mary?" Ooh, Angelica had finally asked the question. Hallelujah! Although, after last night's violence, even I wouldn't expect her to go back there. It was surprising that Angelica was asking the question. What was she up to?

"Were you able to banish the ghost last night?" Mrs Soames asked. "Because when you lot came back in here, you looked right terrified." She pinned me with her gaze and nodded as if to say, Exhibit A.

"I'm afraid not, but you know that because I would have said. What does that letter from the agent say?" Ah, so that's where she was headed. Smart lady, our Angelica.

Each word was reluctantly uttered, if her irritated face was anything to go by. "It's one of those ones they send every now and then, to ask if I'd be interested in selling, that they have buyers waiting."

"Maybe you should consider it. Honestly, Mary, I don't blame you for not wanting to go back, but you can't stay here forever. I'm sorry." Angelica's tone was kind but firm. Mrs Soames was the kind of person who took that mile with every inch you gave her.

Mrs Soames folded her arms. "I don't have anywhere else to go. You think I want to live here?" She rolled her eyes. "I've rung three different churches, and only one of the priests does house visits for hauntings, and he's booked out. Said it's been busy."

"Excuse me a moment." I stood and went to our pile of mail on the counter. Hmm, mobile-phone bill, electricity bill, pizza pamphlet, dog-walking flyer, magnet for a local plumber, but no real-estate agent letter. Hmm…. I returned to the table.

"What was that about?" Olivia asked.

"Um, I'm not sure. Just thinking. I'll let you know later."

She shrugged. "How's the new job going?"

I grinned. "Really well… I think. The work is easy, and I like stickybeaking through other people's homes, but I'm not allowed to talk to the clients if they're there, which is weird, but I can deal."

"So the real-estate industry is currently booming around here, is it?" asked Angelica.

That was an interesting question. "It depends what you mean by booming. It's really busy, but prices aren't great." Which was very strange now that I really thought about it.

Angelica tilted her head to the side and looked at me. "Oh, so there's not many buyers around but lots of sellers?" And that's how supply and demand would work if the market was falling.

"Ah, not exactly. There are lots of sellers, more than usual, but there's lots of buyers too. I don't know. It does seem strange, but, hey, I'm just the photographer." What did I really know about real estate?

"Yes, *just* the photographer." Angelica raised an eyebrow. What did she mean by that?

"Are you working tomorrow?" asked Olivia. "Because I wanted to catch up for lunch. Imani said she can come too. There's this cute French café at Tunbridge Wells I love. Are you in?"

"I've got another two jobs tomorrow morning. I'll be finished by eleven thirty, so, yeah, I'm definitely in." It would be super nice to have a girls' lunch. Fun outings were few and far between around here, and that definitely needed to change.

Angelica's phone rang. It was sitting next to her plate, and I hadn't noticed. That was unusual for her—she was the queen of etiquette, and having your phone on the table was a massive no-no around here. Was she waiting for a call about Will? My mouth went dry, and I put my fork down.

She looked at the screen, then answered it. "Hello, yes." Her gaze darted to me for a moment. My heart rate spiked at the speed of sound. Maybe it was Will? She stood. "Just a moment," she said to whoever it was before saying to us, "Excuse me. I have to take this call." She left the room, her footsteps fading away up the stairs. She was probably headed for her bedroom, or at least somewhere she could travel from in private.

Who the hell was on that call? And more importantly, what did they have to say?

I was going to suffer for the rest of the night not knowing because Angelica never returned to dinner. She sent us a message to put hers in the fridge. Now her spaghetti would be as cold as my long-suffering heart. Okay, so I was being a tad melodramatic, but some slack should be given. The man I cared about was who knew where, doing who knew what, and maybe he wasn't even alive. *No, Lily. Stop*! He's going to be fine. He's not a helpless baby, and he's not stupid. He can take care of himself.

Unfortunately, sometimes that wasn't enough.

CHAPTER 6

O ur run of average, almost-raining weather had finished. All the lights were on in the c. 1960s semi-detached home in Sevenoaks Weald, but it wasn't enough to banish the gloom that leaked in from the charcoal clouds and steady rain falling outside. At least the drumming sound on the roof was comforting, but the comfort came from the implied fact that you could stay indoors and revel in being warm and dry. I was about to dash out into the yard to get my external shots.

When I'd shown up at the first job this morning, Oliver didn't meet me. I'd had to wait ten minutes for another guy, Samuel, to cover for him. Oliver hadn't called in sick—he just hadn't shown, and Samuel had been edgy the whole time, constantly checking his phone or looking out the window.

I made sure my raincoat was done up and my camera

was as protected as it could be, but there was still a chance it would get wet. I guessed now was as good a time as any to use a trickle of magic. I'd been putting it off in case I made myself too tired, or it didn't work, and to be honest, I was more fearful of the second outcome. Funny how avoiding things was so much easier than finding out the truth, which wasn't normal behaviour for me, but I was sure I could learn how to be a master avoider. And in this case, avoiding using my magic meant I was missing out and ultimately shirking my responsibilities. It was time to stop feeling like a victim—it wasn't the universe's choice whether I had my magic back at full power or not; it was mine. I was going to work for it and make it happen no matter what.

No more fear. *Let's do this.*

I focussed on my belly, deep inside where it was raw and tender. When I'd blown up at Mrs Soames, there'd been more heat than normal. Maybe I'd reinjured it? Although, how you injured a portal into yourself, I didn't know. Was it even a portal? There was so much I didn't understand. Gah. I pushed all that unimportant stuff out of the way and delved deep, searching for the golden stream.

There it was. I hesitated before gingerly reaching for it. Warmth filled me, and I smiled as the elephant slid off my back. The weight of failure and loss had been a far heavier burden than I'd realised. It was gone, and I could breathe. Now all I needed to be my light, floaty self was for Will to come back safe and sound.

I stepped outside and shut the door. A thin awning sheltered me from the downpour. I whispered, "Protect my camera from the rain, please." Such a simple spell didn't need to rhyme. I wasn't doing this for the theatrics, and bad luck if I was breaking some witchy code that required us to be poets on top of everything else.

I aimed my lens at the yard and snapped two shots—this was going to need massive editing later for light and colour, but I had my settings on RAW so it would take a large file size—more image to work with. I jogged to the other end of the small yard and stood with my back to the timber-paling fence. Then I took a few more photos. And I was done with not a drop of rain on the lens or camera body. Yay for magic!

When I ran inside, Samuel met me in the living area. "I think it's best if you send me the photos this afternoon. No one can get hold of Oliver." His brow furrowed, and worry seeped from his gaze. Samuel was either a consummate actor or this was way out of character for Oliver. The latter was the most likely, and the whole thing felt... off. Had he run away for some reason, or had someone done something to him?

"Are you going to call the police?"

"His partner's already called them. He left for work this morning but never arrived, which is unlike him, and there's no sign of his car." Samuel ran a hand through his short hair. "Yeah, so send me the photos. If there's any other work for you, I'll send it through."

"Okay, thanks. And I hope Oliver turns up safe and well."

"Thanks."

I let myself out and made a mad dash to the car. I chucked all my equipment in the boot, slammed it shut, and threw myself into the front seat. Rainwater streamed along the gutter, past weeping willows and rounded, chest-high hedges that formed a natural divide between street and house. England was so pretty, even when it wasn't trying. Watching from my car was like living inside an impressionist painting, the scenery blurred by rivulets of rain sliding down my windscreen.

The drive south to Royal Tunbridge Wells took about twenty minutes. I'd briefly visited here before, but I needed Siri's help to find the café. I parked down the road a bit— my habit in the UK. There was always an opportunity to see the sights if I took some time to walk. With my umbrella and raincoat, I'd stay fairly dry.

As I walked along York Road, admiring the rendered brick four-story terraces, someone yelled "Boo!" from just behind me. I jumped and let out a short scream. A woman laughed. "Gotcha!"

I turned. Bloody Imani! "Are you trying to give me a heart attack?"

"Ha, no, love. Just couldn't resist. You knew I was around."

"Yes, but no." I whispered a bubble-of-silence spell. "Whenever anyone was following me before, I could usually make them out. You're exceptionally good at your job. I forgot you were around, and I haven't seen you at all since this 'following me' thing started."

"Lily!" Her mouth dropped open.

"What?" I jerked my head around, looking for the danger.

She lowered her voice—my spell didn't stop normal people from hearing what we were saying. "You're using your magic! That's wonderful. Have you got it back properly, then?"

I smiled. "Yep. At least, I think so. I'm probably going to get tired faster than normal, and I've only tried small spells, but it seems like it. It doesn't feel different to before that… incident, so I'm assuming it's all going to be fine."

She threw her arms around me and squeezed before letting go. "Congratulations."

"Thanks."

She linked her arm through mine. "Let's go. Liv'll be there soon."

We set off. She huddled close to me, sharing my umbrella. "You don't even have a raincoat. What's up with that?"

She shrugged. "Couldn't be bothered."

"You're weird."

She grinned. "Yep."

We turned right at the main road and walked past a hulking sandstone building with three-metre-tall columns at the front. It looked like a cross between Georgian architecture and old Roman or Greek. And there were sale signs out the front. "Is that a clothes shop?"

"Yeah. They've got some good stuff, but a bit expensive."

"That's rather grand for retail. Looks like it should be an

71

art gallery or town hall." Large historical buildings were so few and far between in Sydney that we tended to reserve them for more important things than clothes shops.

"There's lots of grandness around here. You know it used to be where the royals and the well-to-do holidayed, back in the 1800s. It all started because of a chalybeate spring."

"A what?"

She laughed. "It's a spring, you know, water that comes out of the ground, but it has high levels of iron in it."

"Oh, okay. That's one reason to start a town." It didn't take much to get people excited back then. Any reason to start a town. But then again, you did need water to survive, but water containing a lot of iron? Was that even safe to drink?

"Here we are, Côte Brasserie." Imani took a sharp right and opened a glass door. The three-storey building was on a corner. The upper two levels were brownish-coloured bricks, and the ground floor was painted a dark steely blue-grey and had striped awnings protruding over every large window. There was a courtyard at the front with chairs and tables, but no one was out there. Who wanted to eat in the freezing rain? Yeah, not me. She held the door open. I closed my umbrella and stepped inside.

The bright, cheery interior had light-coloured timber floors. A bar section against one wall looked out over the dining area and floor-to-ceiling windows which revealed the courtyard beyond. Olivia waved from a table in the corner to our left.

We both sat, and a waiter came to take our order. He had a sexy French accent, which made him an eight out of ten instead of a five on the attractive scale. I had no idea what made that accent sexy. Accents were strange. Who had originally decided it should be said a certain way? Did they have an agenda, like, "Let's make this sexy, so everyone focusses on our words and wants to sleep with us." In that case, what were they thinking when they invented the Aussie accent? "Let's make it so people think we're happy but rough and maybe a bit simple." Could be good for underestimating us, but other than that, I didn't get it. The British one was clearly contrived so people thought they were the authority on whatever they were talking about. The refined English accent definitely lent gravity to whatever was being said. I was pretty sure they'd done studies on it.

After he took our order, Olivia turned to me. "Argh. When is stupid Mrs Soames going home?"

"You heard her last night. She's not going to go easily. Maybe *we'll* have to move out."

"Is this the woman from across the road with the haunted house?" Imani asked.

"Yes," Liv and I answered at the same time.

"Um, Lily?" a soft voice asked.

I looked up. "Mrs Jennings! Fancy seeing you here." I smiled.

"I work across the road at the museum." She nodded towards the main street.

"Oh, that's right. How's everything going?"

"I'm good, sort of. We've already sold the house. We had

to agree on a price that was lower than we would have liked, but that can't be helped."

"Oh. That's a shame, but I'm glad you sold it so quickly." What the hell? I was only there yesterday. I tried to keep the surprise from my face.

"Yes. Oliver called us with the offer this morning. We went back and forth a couple of times, but we finally agreed on a price."

"Oh, what time was that?"

She looked at me as if to say, that's a bit too personal. But, hey, it wasn't really. "Around eight. Why?"

"I was supposed to meet Oliver at a job this morning, but he didn't turn up. No one's heard from him, but if you spoke to him this morning, he probably just got caught up with something." I had a feeling that meeting her here was the universe's way of giving me an opportunity to find out more, so to keep the "I want to know too much" theme going, I asked, "Are you staying in the area?"

"We're not sure, to be honest. We haven't been looking for long, but there isn't much on the market that doesn't get sold quickly." She looked at her phone. "I have to get back to work, but it was lovely seeing you, and if I speak to Oliver, I'll ask him to call the office. Bye."

She turned and left. Had she even eaten? Olivia frowned. "Why would you sell in a hurry but not have somewhere else to go?"

I shrugged. "I have no idea. And is it just me, or did she just leave rather hastily?"

Imani turned to look out the window. "No, love, it's not just you."

The waiter returned with our drinks. When he left, Olivia said, "You're doing work for Smith & Henderson, right?"

"Mmm hmm."

"Okay, so I have two questions. That flyer Mrs Soames got yesterday was from them, wasn't it?"

I nodded, and my eyes widened. "Yes, and we didn't get one. That's what I was checking our mail for. Which is weird. If you were an agent looking for work, wouldn't you put flyers in everyone's letterbox? Do you think Mrs Jennings's house was haunted, and that's why they're moving?"

"What else would make you leave your house on short notice? It makes total sense. And our houseguest is proof."

"Well, yes and no. I'd never seen a ghost before that one at Mrs Soames's place. What are the chances of having two haunted houses in the same area at the same time?"

Imani tapped the tabletop. "Maybe there's an infestation for some reason? We've just had All Souls' Day."

"Not *just*. That was two weeks ago," Olivia said. Huh? How come they were so up to date on days for the dead? I had no idea about any of that stuff.

Imani pressed her lips together. "Hmm. Maybe the hauntings started then, and the ghosts just never left?"

"You know this is a crazy conversation, right?" I asked. And so was having seen a ghost and almost being injured by it. What had my life become? "Let's suppose you're both right; why would someone jump straight on it and buy it even before it hits the market? Hang on." I googled the listing on my phone, but it wasn't there. I shook my head. "See. It's nowhere."

Imani had a quick look and handed the phone to Olivia. Olivia cocked her head to the side. "Well, agents have a list of buyers who are waiting. Maybe this Oliver guy had the right buyer waiting?"

"We're making a lot of suppositions. You know what? I'm going to go to the museum after lunch to visit Mrs Jennings and ask her about it. What've I got to lose? Oliver said not to talk to the clients during work, but he didn't say anything about me chatting to them out in the wild."

"In the wild?" Imani snorted.

I grinned. "You know what I mean. But seriously, so far, this place has been anything but tame."

We spent an hour chatting and eating. When we were done, Olivia headed back to work, and Imani and I walked across the road to the museum. It was a two-storey brick building, which kind of bland and had a bit of the governments about it. Not nearly as pretty as the massive sandstone structure that housed the clothing shop. They really should swap premises.

The main entry doors led into a double-ceiling-height vestibule. If we went straight ahead, there was the library, and up the stairs was the museum-cum-art gallery. We hurried up the stairs and found Mrs Jennings manning the small reception desk in the first room at the end of the hallway. Imani hung back—we didn't want Mrs Jennings to feel overwhelmed.

As much as I wasn't on the clock right now, if Oliver found out I'd spoken to her, he might never use my services again—that was, if they found where he'd gotten to. "Hi," I said and smiled.

"Oh, Lily. What are you doing here?"

"Um, I'm sorry to bother you, but I needed to ask you something. I realise you may not be comfortable talking about it, but, ah, my neighbour is living with us at the moment because"—I lowered my voice and leaned towards her—"her house is haunted. I never believed in that stuff before, but I've seen it for myself, and it was scary. Is that what happened to you?" If her house hadn't been haunted, she was going to think I was a total loony. Saying it out loud made me rethink what we were doing, but it was too late now.

She stared at me, then snapped her head around, probably checking who was within hearing distance. We were the only two people in here, and Imani was in the hallway just outside. Mrs Jennings shook her head and took a deep breath. "You have to promise not to say anything. I don't want the sale falling through."

I gave her my most earnest expression. "I promise. I'm just trying to figure out if there's something bigger going on, if you know what I mean."

"Look, I don't know if anyone else is going through this, but it started about four weeks ago. There are two ghosts—an angry old lady and naughty child. They manifest at night and wake us up. They've told us to leave. At first, we thought we'd just ride it out; then we got a priest in to bless the house. We tried smudge sticks, telling them to get out, all kinds of things, but nothing worked. For the first week, it was more annoying than anything, but we thought we'd learn to live with it. But then they started to get physical—breaking my cups and plates, levitating kitchen knives, and telling me they were going to kill us." She hugged herself and shivered. "We just couldn't do it anymore. Getting that flyer from Smith & Henderson was a godsend. Oliver's done a wonderful job of finding a buyer."

Gee, I could see wanting to leave and needing to get your money out of it, but did they feel a little bit guilty for just passing the problem onto someone else? And why were all these ghosts so murderous? Not that I ever believed in ghosts before this, but normally the stories are about floating, see-through people who drift in and out and do no more than leave a cold draught or laughter in their wake. This was another level entirely.

"He sure sold it quickly. That must be a record or something." I smiled, trying to make my statement non-threatening.

"I know, but we're so grateful. We did have to drop the price more than we would've liked to make it happen, but we're just happy to be out of there. We'll rent for a while and keep our eye out for something."

"I appreciate you being so candid, Mrs Jennings, and don't worry; I won't say anything to anyone other than my best friend and my aunt—they're worried about our neighbour, and we're not sure what to do. But maybe she'll just have to sell. We'll see."

"I just want this whole thing to be over and done with. Good luck with your neighbour, Lily." She gave me a closed-mouth, half-arsed smile—the smile you give when you're just not feeling it.

"Thanks. You too." I smiled and joined Imani in the hallway. I jerked my head towards the stairs and hurried outside, my friend behind me. Once we were a safe distance from the building, I stopped and spoke in a quiet voice. "She did sell because of a violent ghost—well two, actually—and the agent had a buyer before the home went to market."

"That's odd—about the buyer, not the ghosts."

I drew my brows down. "You don't think the ghosts are odd? I know you said you believed in them, but until the other day, you'd never seen one, and now there're ghosts everywhere. You don't think that's unusual? Because I sure do." If I hadn't been in Mrs Soames's home and confronting the ghost, I never would have believed it either. Since then, I'd been trying to figure out how someone could fake something so real without magic, and I'd come up with nothing.

"You have no explanation for it either. Usually the most obvious answer is the right one."

"Maybe." I still wasn't convinced, but without any evidence, I had to concede ghosts were around. Maybe I was holding onto false hopes that the things that go bump in the night weren't just me running into walls in the dark when I got up at 1:00 a.m. to go to the loo. I shuddered.

"What does it matter to you anyway, Lily? You don't have to solve everyone's problems. Haven't you got enough on your plate right now?"

"I suppose, but we still have to get Mrs Soames out of our house, and she won't leave until that ghost does. Maybe everything's connected somehow, and if I can find an answer, we can get that ghost out of her house, and Mrs Soames can stop haunting us." I giggled. She wasn't murderous, but she was just as bad as a ghost in every other way, and not all ghosts were out to kill. Were they?

Imani grinned. "Fair enough, love, but I haven't got time to run around with you this afternoon. I have to get back to work. Is that okay? Maybe tomorrow we can meet up and figure something out."

"Sounds good." I made a bubble of silence. "Have you heard anything about Will?" She probably wouldn't be able to tell me anything, but I couldn't help asking.

She pouted and gave me a sad face. "I'm sorry, but no." And that was that.

We walked to my car. Just as I was saying goodbye to Imani, my phone rang. "Hello, Lily speaking."

"Hi, Lily. It's Samuel from Smith & Henderson." His voice was hesitant and quiet. I squinted, trying to hear him better, but of course, it didn't help.

"Oh, hi. Is everything okay?"

"I thought I'd better call. I've emailed you three jobs for tomorrow, but we're postponing them for two days."

"Okay. Not a problem." That couldn't be why he sounded on the verge of tears. "Is that all?"

"Um, no, actually. The reason we're postponing is… they've found Oliver—well, his body. I don't know where or what happened, but… yeah."

Crap. My shoulders sagged. His poor family and friends. "I'm so sorry. Is there anything I can do?"

"No, but thanks. Just turn up to those jobs at the same time in three days; that's all."

"Okay. Thanks, Samuel. Again, I'm sorry."

"Yeah. Um, see you soon. Bye."

He hung up before I had a chance to say goodbye. Imani tilted her head to the side, a questioning expression on her face.

"The agent who went missing. He's turned up. Dead."

"Oh," Imani said.

Oh, indeed.

CHAPTER 7

As I'd thought it would, the news that night mentioned Oliver's murder. I had to sit in the TV room with Mrs Soames and her parrot. "Rawrk, murder, rawrk!" If the cockatoo didn't shut up, I wasn't going to hear what the newsreader said. I glared at it, but it bounced up and down as if it were dancing. It had perched on top of the television, so it was more than a little distracting. It bent low, over the screen, and turned its head to the side. Oh, for f—

"Ethel, not in front of the TV." Mrs Soames waved her arm, indicating that Ethel should move. Ethel sat straight, unfurled her wings, madly flapped, and flew to Mrs Soames. A small feather floated to the ground in front of the newsreader's face.

"… body was found in his office by his work colleague, Samuel Murdoch. Police are treating the death as suspicious but haven't released any further details. And now for our next story...."

"Next story, rawrk. Next story."

I stood, my mind wrestling with the news report. Why did Samuel not say he'd discovered the body? Maybe he was in shock, and if the police had told him to keep the information confidential, he might have said it to avoid questions. God knew I wouldn't want to talk about it if I were him. But if Oliver was found in his office, why did it take them most of the day to find him? Surely someone checked there in the morning?

"Thanks, Mrs Soames. You can watch whatever you want." I'd changed the channel to watch the news, and surprisingly, she hadn't complained, which was a first.

"You're welcome. Lily?"

"Yes?"

"Do you think I'll ever get my house back from the ghost, or should I sell?" Her hands were clasped in her lap, and she looked up at me with sad, worried eyes. I sighed. She was so prickly that it was easy to forget she was probably just as put out as we all were, and she missed her home. It must be torture to go outside and see the house she couldn't live in, a house filled with memories of a life shared with her husband and kids.

"I'll be honest with you, Mrs Soames. It's hard for all of us to be living together, and I wish you could get back into your house sooner rather than later, but I know it's not possible right now, and as much as I'd like to see you resolve this issue, I don't think you should sell. We're still working on getting rid of the ghost, so maybe give us another week or two. I know it's hard not to have your own place to go to, but I think selling right now would be a mistake."

"How do you know it would be a mistake?" There was no snark in her tone, just genuine curiosity, which was another surprise. She must be worn out from being so cranky over the last few days.

"I have a gut feeling. I really have no proof, but I think there's more to this than what we realise." I had no idea what the connection between hauntings, house sales, and Oliver's murder was, but there must be one. I wasn't much for coincidences explaining everything away.

"Okay, Lily. I'll wait. Thanks for your honesty."

"My pleasure. I'll let you know if I figure it out." I gave her a smile and headed to the kitchen—it was time to cook dinner. Home-made pizza was on the menu. My stomach grumbled. *Yeah, yeah, settle down. I'll feed you soon.*

I'd just finished putting toppings on and was slipping the second pizza in the oven when Angelica said, "Good evening, Lily. Cooking dinner, I see."

I jumped, and my breath came in pants. *Bloody hell. I swear I'm going to just drop dead from a heart attack one of these days.* "Jeez, don't sneak up on me!"

She raised her brows. "I did no such thing. I came in the front door and walked in here like a normal person."

"You are *not* a normal person, and you walk as quietly as a ninja. Maybe stomp down the hall next time so I have some warning."

"Maybe you need to take relaxation classes, dear. Meditation is good for the soul and for avoiding heart attacks."

I scrunched my face up. I'd forgotten my mind-shield again. Now I had my magic back, I needed to remember to protect my thoughts. It took me ages to get into the habit the first time around, and this time was no different.

"Yes, dear. You really need to get back into the habit." She grinned.

I narrowed my eyes. *Maybe you should do the polite thing and stay out of my brain.*

"No need to get testy, dear." Gah, why didn't Angelica have boundaries?

I mumbled my thought-protection spell. Finally, my thoughts were my own.

She folded her arms and looked down her nose at me. "See, that didn't take much effort, did it?" And just like that, she was the teacher, and I was eight again and getting in trouble for something that wasn't even my fault.

"No, but how much effort would it have taken for you not to eavesdrop?" Gah, why was I so angry? Maybe I was just frustrated about the Mrs Soames thing and the Will-being-missing thing. "Sorry. I'm just not in the mood for complications, or for getting surprised half to death. How was your day?"

"Probably about as good as yours. She leaned towards me and lowered her voice to a whisper. "I need you to come into work. The case with that agent has been referred to us. Evidence of magic use was found at the scene."

"Could it have been someone from his office, I mean, just using it for filing or something?"

"No witches work there. We have a couple of our agents down there collecting evidence now. Can you pop in tomorrow morning at nine?"

"Yeah, sure." I didn't have anything on now those other jobs were postponed for a day. As nice as it would've been to have a day off, it was better to keep busy. The less time I had to think about Will, the better. Was he with *the evil one* right now? Had he forgotten me, or was he only doing it in a professional capacity? What if he had to sleep with her? Nausea slithered up my throat. A wave of hot tears filled my eyes. If he slept with her, would I be able to take him back?

"Lily, are you all right?" Angelica stared at me, her brow furrowed, just like Will's normally was.

And that, folks, was the proverbial straw.

Salty morsels of anguish surged over my hastily constructed dam walls. No amount of tongue biting or distraction would stop the flood. And I hated crying in front of people, so I ran upstairs to my room, where I could have my mini-breakdown in private.

I lay on my bed in a hopeless blah of sniffles and tears. There was a good chance Will was dead, and if he even was still alive, there was an even better chance he'd fallen back in love with Piranha, if indeed he'd ever fallen out of love with her. As percentages went, my shot at happiness with him had gone from a pre-mission high of around 90 percent to an all-time low of about 10 percent. Who would be stupid enough to take those odds?

That would be me and my foolish friend Hope. Hope and I had been close for a long time. She didn't normally steer me in the wrong direction, but this time, I feared her enthusiasm was going to end in more tears... and they'd all be mine.

CHAPTER 8

Sitting at the conference table at the PIB was both a comfort and a torture—I was among my best friends, but one important person was missing—He Who Shall Not Be Named for fear I'd cry.

Beren sat on one side of me, and Olivia the other. They were so sweet. I knew they would have preferred to sit next to each other, but they wanted me to feel the love. And feel it, I did, but it wasn't enough to banish the melancholy. James and Imani sat opposite me, and Ma'am filled her spot at the head of the table, as per usual. Millicent was absent— incubating a baby was hard work, and she had a few things to finish at home before the baby came.

Ma'am—it was hard to think of her as Angelica at work —folded her hands in front of her on the table as she ran through the case. "So, the magic signature we found was faint, as if they'd tried to make it fade. Whoever did this obviously didn't want anyone to know witches were involved, but, thankfully, no one has worked out how to wipe magic signatures away. Time is the only thing that will do that, although if we'd gotten to this in a few days, it would have been gone. They probably thought they'd get away with not being discovered because they've made it look like suicide."

A piece of paper appeared on the table in front of each of us. Angelica gave a nod. "This is the suicide note Oliver supposedly left. His boyfriend and his personal assistant have confirmed it's in his handwriting. Please take a moment to read it."

We all did as asked.

The pressure has been too much. I'm sorry it's come to this, but I can't go on. I'm sorry I failed you, Tim. You'll be better off without me. Please move on—I want you to be happy.

To my workmates, you know you're better at this than I am. Now you're free to take the business to the next level. Yours in failure, Oliver P Smith.

Short but not so sweet.

I looked up at Ma'am. "Other than the magic at the scene, how do we know it wasn't suicide?"

Ma'am turned to me. "I'm glad you asked, dear. For one, according to those who knew him best, his sentiment didn't ring true. He was confident, successful, and had no reason to think he was a failure."

"But doesn't depression make the person lie to themselves? You know, make you think the worst things about yourself that aren't true?" It was also a silent killer—loved ones were usually the last to know the person was suffering.

"Yes, Lily, but he had never suffered from depression in the past, and there is no medical or behavioural history that indicates he's ever had it. We also have a test for it, thanks to Beren." She smiled at her nephew. "We tested blood samples, and there was no trace of the chemicals emitted during depression. Also, his other neurological chemicals were balanced."

Okay, if she said so, I'd have to take it as fact, and if the test results stood up in court, who was I to argue?

"He died by drug injection. A massive dose of pure heroin. According to friends and family, he has never used drugs, and it was clear there were no other needle marks anywhere on his person."

"So, whoever set this up wasn't very smart?" I couldn't help asking. I mean, wouldn't they do their homework?

"That's one way to look at it," Ma'am said. "What I believe they were thinking is that they just had to fool the regular police for a week, and once the magic signature was gone, there would be nothing else to prove it wasn't suicide. The other reason—the one that is more than worrying—is that they just didn't care. Someone wanted Oliver Smith out of the way, and whether or not people thought it was suicide didn't matter, and maybe they wanted to let off a warning shot to someone else. Fear is a wonderful way to keep others in line, and their arrogance hasn't gone unnoticed by the PIB."

That didn't sound good. "So whoever did this thinks the PIB can't touch them because they're too clever?"

"Pretty much," said James. My brother had been quietly nodding as Ma'am made her points. "Lucky for us, an inflated sense of their own intelligence and infallibility is likely a sign that they're actually not very smart." He smirked. "Stupid people don't know what they don't know."

Imani spoke up. "Do we know who they were trying to warn?"

Ma'am answered. "Because it happened at work, we're assuming they intended someone from the real-estate office to take note. And we're betting that person is the one who found the body."

"Samuel?" I asked.

Ma'am smiled and nodded. "James will outline how we're to proceed."

"Thank you, Ma'am." He looked at Olivia. "We've confiscated Oliver's laptop and all the paperwork we could find, going back twelve months; however, there's a lot missing. In particular, the last four months' worth of files. His assistant claims she knows nothing about where they are and said she doesn't remember seeing any new paper-work in that time. She does admit that's highly unusual. Our conclusion is that her memory has been tampered with. I'd like you to go through what we've got, but I also want you to find out all the properties Oliver's sold in the time that's missing. If someone's bought them, there should be government records, maybe even an Internet advertising footprint, that sort of thing. I want a list of every property transaction he's facilitated in the last six months."

Liv nodded. "Okay. I'll get onto it today."

"Great." He smiled, then turned his gaze to me. "I'm glad you have your magic back." He grinned. "Because we're going to need it. I want you and Beren to go to their offices and take some photos, see what you can find."

I opened my mouth to protest that Samuel knew who I was and that I'd lose their work, but James was one step ahead. "Yes, Lily, I know you've been working for them, but they're non-witches, so I'm going to get our specialist glamour maker to spell you before you go. By the time she's finished, you'll look nothing like yourself."

"Ah, okay. If you say so. Do I get to choose what I look like?" Hmm, maybe I could get them to make me five foot ten, skinny, and with elegant, feline-like movements. It would be cool to be a supermodel for five minutes.

"To an extent. She won't change height or body shape— that's possible but takes too much magic. While she's holding your spell together, she won't be able to give her power to anyone else. We'll be changing your facial features and giving you a wig."

"A wig? That's not very magical. Since when is the PIB old school?"

James frowned. "I wish you'd take this more seriously, Lily."

My cheeks heated. I was taking it seriously, but I needed to make a joke every now and then, or stress would get the better of me, and shame on him for not knowing that. As my brother, he should be aware of my coping mechanisms. "I am. Don't worry."

James narrowed his eyes. Trusting me was obviously hard for him. Brothers—who needed them? Not me, right now. "Right, well, after you and Beren take those photos, you're going to visit a couple of local priests."

Ma'am interrupted. "This is to cover the theory we had, Lily. We want to know whether the hauntings have anything to do with this. It's our most obvious conclusion, so best to confirm or dispense with it before we go too far into the investigation. If the haunting theory doesn't pan out, we'll consider our next option, which might have everything to do with who is buying these properties if, indeed, it's only one person, or only people closely related to the selling agent." Ma'am looked at Imani. "I want you to go with James and interview Samuel again. After that, you can help Olivia here. I may send you out with Beren and Lily later, depending on where we decide to go after they've checked out the ghost angle. If anyone has any questions, direct them to James. I have meetings for the rest of today." She stood. "Thanks for your time, everyone. We'll reconvene here tomorrow afternoon at five."

Rather than make a doorway, she left the normal way. Her meetings were probably in the building. Olivia and Beren stood and walked to the door together, having a private chat. I smiled. When were they going to go on their first date? It was about time, really. Life was way too short, and anything could happen. I sighed and tried not to think of what Will might be doing right this moment. Gah.

James got up and came around the table. "Hey, sis. Congrats on the return of your magic."

I stood, and we hugged. "Thanks, bro." I grinned.

We dropped the hug, and he regarded me with serious eyes. "How's everything else?"

"If by everything else, you mean the Will situation? About as shitty as you'd imagine. Not knowing anything is driving me batty. Is he alive, and if he is, does he even… you know…?" I sighed and let the sadness settle around me.

"I'm sorry I can't tell you anything, but hang in there. I have to believe things will work out for the best… whatever happens. And I'm here for you, so is Mill. We love you, kiddo. Never forget that." He grabbed my hand and gave it a squeeze. "I have a feeling you're going to be the best auntie ever." He grinned.

I couldn't help but smile. I wished my parents could be here for that moment, but even so, it was going to be pure joy to meet my niece or nephew for the first time. "I can't wait. And thanks. I know you guys care, but this relationship stuff is something I have to go through alone. No one can help. Maybe just distract me."

"I'll do my best to keep you busy. If you need anything, let me know."

"Will do." He gave me another quick hug, then turned to Imani. "Okay, ready?"

"Yes, boss." She smiled. "Let's go."

They both made a doorway and left. Which meant I was alone with the two dreamy-eyed ones. Beren and Olivia grinned at each other, not saying much, but neither one wanting to leave. Ordinarily I would bask in the cuteness, but it made me think of Will and what we didn't have. I pouted. Gah! I had to stop thinking about it. Talk about unproductive.

I cleared my throat. "Ah, sorry to break up your love sesh, but we've got work to do." I smirked.

Olivia blushed and stared at me, her mouth open. "You did *not* just say that!"

I laughed. "Yep, I'm pretty sure I did. I'd say get a room, but we don't have time for that."

Beren's eyes were huge. Did he think their attraction had gone unnoticed? He recovered with a lopsided grin. "All in good time." He turned and winked at Liv, and she bit her lip.

"Awesome. Maybe go out on a date or something… after work. Now, let's go, B."

"Hey, that's a great idea!" He kissed Liv on the cheek. "Dinner tonight? How does Shamrat at Maidstone sound?"

She grinned. "Perfect."

"I'll pick you up at seven." He leaned down and gave her a quick peck on the lips. *Finally!* Although I wasn't sure if it was a good or bad thing. Now I probably had to put up with him all dopey happy for the afternoon. Oh well. It was a small price to pay for the happiness of my friends. Beren looked at me. "Okay, we can go now. We'll go to Roxanne, the disguise specialist. Then we'll take a PIB car to the real-estate agent's."

We walked with Liv as far as the lift. She kept going, and

we got in. When the doors closed, I nudged Beren. "Smooth."

"Hey, are you hassling my dating prowess?"

"Took you long enough. Why?"

He shrugged. "Every time I thought of asking her, I imagined her saying no, and I chickened out."

Oh my God. This guy was tall, handsome, nice, smart, and had the sexiest green eyes ever, and he was doubting whether she'd want to date him? Not to mention the way Liv always looked at him. "Honestly, B, dare I say it, but you're a hot guy, and Liv's been drooling over you for weeks. But don't tell her I told you, or she'll kill me." I laughed.

He stared at me. "If I'm so hot, why didn't you like me back when we first met?"

The lift stopped, and we got out. Oh, um…. How to be honest yet considerate? "I did, but I liked Will more. I'm sorry. But just think, if we'd dated, you would've missed out on Liv."

He smiled. "You're right. Liv's a gorgeous girl, and we clicked the first time we met. And it's cool that you and I are friends, because we'll never have a messy breakup."

Which brought me back to thinking about you know who. I sighed. Beren scrunched his face up. "I'm sorry, Lily." He mumbled the bubble-of-silence spell. "You know he cares about you, right? He would never ever choose anyone over you, especially not that evil witch. Before he left, he asked me to look out for you, and I haven't done a very good job of that. Sorry." He looked so sad with his down-turned mouth, and the sparkle had left his eyes.

"Hey, don't worry. None of this is your fault, and I was hibernating too. It's not like I reached out to you. There's nothing anyone can do to fix this, except wait. You're a good friend, B. I just want you to be good to Liv and be happy."

He smiled. "I can do that, but I can also be a better friend to you." He gave me a quick hug. "I'm worried about him too, but I just try not to think about it."

"Okay, enough talk about Will. Let's go change this face." I gestured to said face. Roxanne's office wasn't really an office—more a lab. It was a large room with grey vinyl-tile floors, white walls, and two stainless-steel tables. It kind of looked like an autopsy room, to be honest. The only difference was the double row of white busts lined up along a stainless-steel benchtop that ran along one wall. A wig sat atop each bust.

A short, slim, white-coat clad woman with large round glasses and curly brown hair met us just inside the door. She smiled. "Hey, Agent DuPree. Long time no see." I stifled a giggle at the rhyme. Yep, I was such a child. "And who do we have here?"

Beren gestured towards me. "This is Lily, Agent Bianchi's sister. Did Ma'am tell you we were coming?"

"Ah, yes, early this morning." She turned to me. "I understand we just have to make you not look like you."

"Yep. That's about it."

"Do you have any preferences as to how you'd like to look?"

I shrugged. I could just leave it up to her, or I could reinvent myself. It could be fun if I let it be. Hmm.... It also gave me ideas for something else, but I'd talk to Ma'am about that later. Pretending to be someone else could make getting information from people easy, although it wasn't a long-term thing. "How long can you keep me looking like someone else?"

"It depends how busy we are. I work with one other agent, and between us, we can keep three agents disguised at a time, but we need a break to sleep and rest. It takes a lot of concentration and power loss. We also can't keep disguises fed every day, or we'd burn out."

"Gee, it sounds a lot tougher than I thought. I'll only need thirty minutes of disguise, so I won't tax you too much. Can you make me look like a man?"

Beren's eyes widened, and he laughed. "You're kidding, right?"

"Why not? It's something different."

"Um, very." He shook his head.

Roxanne smiled. "I can definitely do that. Let's start by picking a wig, and I can work around that."

I grabbed a dark brown wig that was short at the back and sides with a longer, spiked-up fringe. It was a bit rock star. Roxanne put my hair in a flattish bun, pinned up the stray bits, and put a hairnet around the whole thing, then pretty much shoehorned my skull into the wig. I looked into the mirror above the wigs. Since I didn't wear make-up, I was already looking boyish.

"Sit here, please." Roxanne indicated a dentist-style chair at the far side of the room.

I settled into it. "This won't hurt, will it?"

She smiled. "Not at all. I won't actually be changing your features. What I do is a combination of magical make-up overlaid with a reality spell so that anyone who sees you will immediately accept the magical features they're seeing. It doesn't always work on witches because the spell has a faint orange glow, which ends up looking like bad fake tan to a witch. It's a complete giveaway." That was good to know. If I ever saw anyone super orange, I would be on guard, unless it was Donald Trump, of course. He was just orange.

Roxanne settled her fingers on my face and pushed my cheeks, gently pinched my nose, and mumbled. It was as if she were sculpting clay, but then I had to close my eyes because watching her fingers was making me cross-eyed and nauseous. Her magic warmed my skin, prickling uncomfortably at times. After a few minutes, the tingle of magic disappeared, although my skin was still warmer than normal, kind of like I had sunburn.

"There. I'm done."

I opened my eyes. Roxanne and Beren stood next to the chair, staring at me and nodding. Beren's lips were pressed together as if he were saying "Hmm" in a positive, this-could-work way.

"Can I see?" I really wanted to see what they saw. My foot jiggled with impatience.

Roxanne smiled. "Of course." She nodded at the mirror.

I swivelled around, slid off the chair, and stood in front of the mirror.

Oh my.

I did have a distinct orange glow, but I also had brown eyes, a stronger jawline, impressive pecs where my boobs had been, and three-day growth. Dare I say it, but I was kinda cute. I'd date me. I laughed. "Nice job, Roxanne. Thank you!"

She grinned. "Thank you. I'll link my power to it for an hour. If you need longer, get Beren to call me. Oh, and I forgot something." She wrapped her hand around my throat and said, "The voice that was high should now be low. It's a man who's talking; these looks aren't just for show." She dropped her hand. "Say something."

Why is it that talking normally posed no problem, but as soon as someone asked you to speak, well, there was nothing to say. "I'm Lyle. Pleased to meet you." My mouth dropped open. That bass rumble was me? Oh my God, how weird. I turned to the mirror again. It was beyond strange to see the me that wasn't me and didn't even sound like me. Who was I? With the gender-neutral clothes I'd worn today—black jeans, hiking boots, and a green long-sleeve T-shirt—I looked every inch the man. Oh, wow. I didn't have that, did I? I cupped the front of my jeans and breathed out. Phew!

Beren snorted, and Roxanne laughed. "Don't worry, Lily," she said. "I would never go that far. It's just illusion, remember?" She winked.

My arms filled out my top nicely. I flexed my bicep in the mirror.

Beren shook his head. "It's disturbing, but you make a good-looking man. I don't know if I'll ever be able to see you the same way again." He chuckled.

I giggled, which sounded ridiculous with my deep voice. As much as I missed Will, I was glad he wasn't here to see me like this. If he saw me as a man, he might never sleep with me again, um, not that we'd slept together in the first place. If he came back unsullied by Piranha, I would remedy that quick smart—life was too short to wait for things that were meant to be. It was sad that it was the first time I was glad he wasn't here. But he'd be back eventually —I just had to believe it.

"I guess I'd better go take some photos." I magicked my Nikon to my hand, which looked a bit bigger than normal and, ew, hairier. Maybe this wasn't such a great idea.

Beren turned to Roxanne. "Thanks, Roxy. You've done an outstanding job with our lad here. We'll see you later."

"Bye." I slammed my mouth shut, waved, and followed Beren out the door. It was going to take some time to get used to my different voice. As we walked to the lift and got in, Beren kept giving me side-eyed glances. I snorted. "Fancy me, do you?"

He blushed. "Ah, no. It's just disconcerting. I like you better as a woman."

"I'm taking that as a massive compliment since I'm such a hot guy." I winked and ran my hand over his chest.

He grabbed my wrist and pushed it away. "Now you're just being creepy, Lyle." He laughed. "You need a boy's name if we're going to do this properly."

"I'm offended by your rejection, B. We could be so good together." I made kissy noises.

He snorted. "Sorry, I don't swing that way, buddy. Oh,

look, the basement." The doors opened, and he jumped out. I laughed. He was really taking my transformation seriously, but I was still the same person underneath it all.

Beren stopped walking at a red Porsche. Nice car, but…. "Um, isn't this a bit conspicuous?" Not that I was against gorgeous sports cars, but people were going to stare.

"Sometimes it's best to hide in plain sight. Besides, I enjoy cruising around in a Porsche." He got in the driver's side and left me to open my own door. Hmm, one point against being a man—normally he would've opened the door for me. I fell into the low car—not too elegant an entrance, but now I was a guy, it probably didn't matter.

The smell of leather and the way the seat hugged me as I settled back wasn't too shabby. Okay, maybe there was something to this. Or was that the guy in me talking?

As we drove to the agent's, my parents came to mind. They'd been driving a Porsche in one of my photos when they'd visited Churchill's house. "Do the PIB have a lot of Porsches?"

"A fair few. I think we have some deal with them. The general manager's a witch, and we solved a big case for them going on fifteen years or so. I wasn't around then, of course, but Angelica knows all about it. They give us a nice discount on them. Not that they get driven that much because of *travelling*." I would admit that cruising around in a Porsche was much nicer than making a doorway to a toilet cubicle, but travelling was way more convenient.

"What happens to them when the PIB doesn't need

them anymore?" Maybe if I could find the one my parents had been driving, I'd find some clues.

"I have no idea. Maybe they sell them, or maybe we still have them somewhere? You'd have to ask my aunt."

"Okay, thanks." It could be a waste of time, but then again, a game-changing clue might turn up.

About ten minutes later, we arrived at the real-estate office. Beren parked in a back street, and we walked to the main road. A teenager—she must have been about seventeen—with blonde hair and slim figure gave me the once-over, staring at me until we'd passed each other. Beren snorted. "Oh, you got game. You gonna ask her out?"

I laughed. "Apparently I wasn't joking when I said I was hot. I think I'm a hotter guy than girl. Men don't stare at me like that on the street, not that I want them to." It was nice to walk around fairly inconspicuously. When I was about that other girl's age, I'd get wolf-whistled every time I went for a run. It was so annoying and creepy. Reaching the ripe old age of twenty-four must mean I was too old for that kind of attention. Too funny.

Beren opened the door for me, and we went straight to the reception desk, which sat in front of a partition that hid the rest of the office. A young woman in a white shirt and grey suit jacket looked up from what she was doing on her desktop. She smiled. "Can I help you?"

I let Beren take the lead since he was the actual agent. Because we were dealing with non-witches, we had to give our alternate job descriptions, and I'd likely stuff it up. "I'm Officer DuPree. I'm from the Kent Special Police. My boss has arranged for us to take some more photos of Mr Smith's office." He gave her a considered smile—one that wasn't too happy, under the circumstances, but one which implored her to trust him and that we wouldn't be here if we didn't have to be. Almost an apology for bringing up Oliver's death.

Her face fell, and her eyes glistened. She nodded. "Of course, of course." She stood. Her chair banged against the partition, and her mouth dropped open as if she'd been startled by the noise. She shook her head. "Sorry. We're all still upset by what's happened. Olly was such a great boss, and he was so nice. I just can't believe he's gone." She carefully used one fingertip to wipe a tear from her eye, so as not to smudge her make-up, I was guessing.

She led us behind the partition and down the narrow space between the rows of desks lined up against both walls. There were four partitioned desks on each side. At the end of that section, the corridor continued, passing two doors on either side. I figured the kitchen and toilet areas were at the end, but we stopped at one of the doors that had police tape across it. "We're not allowed in there yet, so I guess you just go in." She gave a half smile and went back the way we came.

Beren opened the door. We stepped under the tape, and I shut the door behind us. Oliver's office had dark blue carpet, a timber desk with a desktop computer on it, a plush chair behind it with three comfy-looking guest chairs in front of it. Against the wall to the right of the desk were built-in cupboards which went to hip height. On the timber top was a row of books, which were bookended by gold-coloured trophies. I had to assume it wasn't real gold because you'd lock that up. Or you'd sell them and buy yourself a small island.

Beren must have noticed me looking. "He won UK real-estate agent of the year for their company two years running."

"Nice. How do they work it out? Is it revenue or how professional and pleasant they are to clients?"

Beren shrugged. "Knowing the world we live in, he probably turned over the most money or sold the most properties for the franchise." Depressingly, that made sense. "But we're not here to look at that."

"But what if someone killed him because they were jealous?"

Beren raised a brow. "For someone who doesn't want to be an agent, you sure are thinking like one. We've asked about anyone who had it in for him, and other than one old man who was unhappy with the price he got for his house two years ago, there wasn't anyone. Which is pretty rare, actually."

"Not everyone who hates someone makes their feelings known. What's that saying? Keep your friends close and your enemies closer? It would be easier to hurt someone if you had access to their life, which you wouldn't if they were being wary of you."

"True, but still, we've looked into all his contacts, and we're just not seeing it. Let's stop wasting time and take some photos. What you find could stop a lot of conjecture." He raised both brows as if to say, "You know I'm right."

I took the lens cap off and flicked the camera on. I knew my magic had returned, but nervousness fluttered in my chest. What if it wasn't always back? Or what if it had changed somehow, and I was yet to find out? I took a deep breath. *Calm yourself, woman.*

I lifted the camera to my face. "Show me who killed Oliver." Nothing. Hmm. "Show me the moment Oliver died." Nope. He didn't appear. So he *was* killed somewhere else. That was a start. "Show me the moment Oliver arrived dead in the office." His body appeared on the floor behind his desk, his legs sticking out the side—they were the only things I could see from where I stood.

I clicked a shot, walked close and clicked again, then went all the way around the desk and took a few more shots. But that was it. Nothing to see here, folks. I got the photos on the screen and handed the camera to Beren. "Whoever killed him sent him here with magic. There's no other expla- nation." Beren had heard my questions, so he could tee them up with the photos and draw his own conclusions.

"Looks like it."

"Now what?" This seemed like a dead end, but I didn't want to give up—that wasn't my way. Beren pressed his lips together, but before he could figure out what we could do, I remembered something from the meeting. "Didn't Ma'am say there were files missing? Maybe I could look for those with my camera?"

"That's a great idea!"

"Show me all the files that have been in here the last four months." I looked through the lens. Nothing. Huh? I walked around the table and stood facing his desktop computer. Blank, dark, turned off. I turned my camera off. "Sorry, B. Nothing."

"We haven't searched his home office because the official line was that it was suicide, even though we've put the crime-scene tape on this office door—we told his staff that we just wanted to be sure and didn't want his office contaminated until we'd finished."

"Can you use the same reasoning with the home office?"

"If his partner didn't want to let us in, we couldn't get a warrant. We don't have enough evidence to say it was murder."

Damn. We really did have nothing. Having nothing sucked big time. Frustration boiled in my gut. I made a bubble of silence. "Maybe we'll figure out something when Olivia's done her research. I can't help thinking this haunting thing has something to do with all those properties he's sold lately. They've been selling really quickly, and one of the ones I went to, the woman admitted she was getting out because it was haunted. And then there's Mrs Soames from across the road. Her house is horribly haunted, and then she gets a letter from this agency asking if she's looking to sell."

"I don't know. That's a massive conclusion to draw from two bits of information. When Olivia's done, maybe we can interview the vendors and ask them. We'll soon see whether there's a pattern." At least he was willing to entertain my idea.

"Cool. Well, I guess we're done here."

"Yep, buddy." He clapped me on the shoulder. "Anything you'd like to do for the last thirty minutes of being a man?"

I grinned. "Take over the world?"

He laughed. "I have a feeling you could do that, no matter what gender you were."

"Does that mean I can count you in as a minion?"

He smiled. "Definitely. You can always count on me. You know that, right?"

"Yep, B. I know, and thanks. Same here. You do know this is a weird place to be having a deep and meaningful conversation?" Standing in a room where there had recently been a dead body wasn't a great place for doing anything, really.

We walked back out to the reception area. The receptionist sniffed and tried to smile through her tears. She blew her nose into a tissue. "Sorry. I shouldn't be crying at work; it's just that…."

I made my tone as empathetic as possible, which was hard since I didn't recognise my own voice. "It's okay. We understand. He was obviously someone everyone liked."

"You can say that again." She gave a nod to all the flower arrangements on a table sitting against one wall. Wow, there were twelve. "And that's not even all of them. We've moved some to his house and some to a local nursing home. We've had over eighty bunches of flowers and cards from clients and colleagues."

"Well, we're sorry he's gone." I didn't know what else to say. It was hard enough with people you knew. There was nothing good to say when someone died. It was just a shitty thing. I guess being kind was a good place to start, but whatever you did or said always felt inadequate because the only thing that really mattered—bringing the person back—was impossible. I sighed as sorrow muffled my happiness.

We said goodbye and left. When we got in the car, I turned to Beren. "We need to figure this out. So many people loved him. It's only fair that we punish whoever did this. The murderer has affected so many people, not just Oliver. Why can't solving crimes be easier?"

Beren started the car. "I don't know, Lily. But we'll do whatever we can to make sure we get to the bottom of this. Okay?"

As we drove back to the PIB, I hoped that would be enough.

CHAPTER 9

Later that afternoon, after we'd tried to visit two priests—they'd both been out—Beren left to investigate a different crime, and I returned to the PIB to help Olivia. While we compiled a list of vendors to interview, Ma'am walked into Millicent's office, which was probably Olivia's office now that Millicent would be off work for a few months. "Good afternoon, ladies."

"Hi," we answered in unison. My "hi" had been cheerful, but that sentiment soon disappeared. Ma'am had her poker face on, which meant she was here to tell us something boring or unpleasant.

"Thank you for the photos, Lily. We have a more concrete direction now that we know for sure magic is involved. It was disappointing you didn't photograph the killer, but it can't be helped."

I bit my tongue. Responding with "It wasn't my fault"

wouldn't help. And if her rigid posture was any indication, there was more to come.

She lifted her hand and gave me an envelope. "This came for you yesterday. I collected it with my mail and only discovered this morning it wasn't for me." Which was fair since nothing ever came for me. My phone bills came via email, and with messaging apps, none of my Aussie friends wrote letters. I took the envelope, curious. Oh, she'd already opened it.

As I slid the letter out, Ma'am stared down at me. Was she awaiting my reaction? I unfolded the thick cream-coloured page—expensive stationery. Was the Queen inviting me to tea? I snorted. Ma'am scowled. Whatever was in here obviously was no snorting matter. "Do I really want to read this?"

"No, but you're going to have to." She mumbled and moved her hand to indicate she was casting a bubble of silence.

I wrinkled my forehead. Was this about my parents? Surely she'd warn me first if it were super-bad news? I swallowed and read aloud, so Olivia wouldn't feel left out.

DEAREST LILY, I HOPE THIS NOTE FINDS YOU RECOVERED AFTER *your recent near-death experience. Please be careful and take care of yourself. You're more valuable than you know. And be more patient with poor Mrs Soames; she's just a non-witch after all. Until we finally meet.*

Yours in anticipation,

Mr X.

A SHIVER SKITTERED ALONG MY ARMS AND DOWN MY SPINE. A creepy undertone ran beneath every line, not to mention this person knew way too much about what was going on in my life. But Mr X? How cheesy. Was he trying to be funny? "Do you know who it is?" I asked Ma'am.

"No. Do you?"

"No. Is there a magic signature or fingerprints?"

"No magic signature, no prints, no DNA."

"Should I be worried?" I was pretty sure no matter her answer, my daily level of worry would certainly increase from an eight to a nine, maybe a ten.

Rather than immediately reassure me, Ma'am sized me up. "No more worried than you normally are. We already have Imani tailing you, and you have your magic back. There's not much else we can do, and by the sounds of it, this person doesn't want to hurt you."

"But they want something from me, and I'd bet it's something they know I won't want to give. And they want me to be scared, or why the cryptic note. They could have signed their real name. Could it be from the snake group?"

"Yes, but we don't want to assume too much. There could be someone else out there watching you as well. We can't be too careful."

Great, just great. Olivia shared a worried glance with me. "So someone's been spying on me?"

"It looks that way. I've checked the protective wards

around the house, and nothing's been breached. Maybe whoever's spying on you has approached Mrs Soames when she's been at the shops, had a seemingly innocent conversation with her?" Ma'am sat in one of Millicent's guest chairs. "The fact that you had a near-death experience could have been leaked by anyone at the PIB."

"Two agents in particular." I folded my arms and slumped back in my chair.

"Yes, dear, but don't discount innocent conversations. Word gets around. It's called gossip." She smirked. "Not many people are above that in the workplace, I'm sorry to say. While I'm here, I may as well ask how your investigation is going."

Olivia smiled—this was really her domain, so she could answer. "I've uncovered details for twenty-five sales going back ten–twelve weeks ago. I'll need more time to get the rest, and anything within the last month or so probably hasn't gone through the government records yet. All but one of the properties were bought by companies—not the same company, though. Which means our next step is to look up company records."

I leaned forward. "Do we have the vendor names? Beren and I need to interview them and find out why they sold. I have a feeling they'll all have a similar story to tell."

"Righto, ladies. Sounds like you have this all in hand." Ma'am stood. "If you find anything else, please inform James. I'll see you later." She walked out the normal way.

I was sitting next to Olivia at her table that was at a T to Millicent's. She typed something into the computer. "Can we get a printout of vendors and purchasers' details? I can start investigating with B."

"For sure. I'll have to order searches for each company, though. Why don't you start with this one first?" She pressed Print, and the machine in the corner buzzed away, then spat out a sheet. I stood and grabbed it. It was the sale to the only non-company purchaser. The buyer was Orwell Sampson. Cool name. "Can we find out the purchaser's new address or their phone number?"

"Possibly, but if they only have a mobile number, it won't help. Let me see if I can find something." As she typed, I went to one of the two windows and gazed out. The PIB buildings were surrounded by parkland and two-metre high fencing topped with barbed wire. It was a sprawling site filled with large trees and more than one pond. Ducks waddled below, and squirrels—I whispered a little "squee"—zipped around, fossicking for whatever food they could find. A woman, who'd been sitting on the park bench near the lake, stood and shook out what looked to be a container, sending small bits of her lunch to the grass. When she turned and walked towards the building, three of the squirrels hurried over and picked up her scraps. At least someone was thinking about the squirrels. I should go down later and give them something.

Olivia giggled. "Admiring the squirrels again, are we?"

I grinned. "But of course. Ain't nothing cuter than a squirrel squirreling."

"I don't know. Otters are pretty adorable when they're

floating around holding hands, or paws, or whatever it is they have."

"True, but they're not consistently as cute."

"Says you. I beg to differ."

"Squirrel hater."

She sucked in a loud breath. "I am not! Bite your tongue, missy!"

I laughed. It was almost as if everything was all right in our world. But reality, as always, had to intrude. The printer buzzed again. "Do you want to grab that?" Olivia asked.

"Sure." It was for me, after all. I grabbed the page and read. "Oh, cool, their forwarding address is a shop in Westerham. "Clive's Tarts." I sniggered. "I hope that's a pastry shop."

Liv giggled. "Yes, it is. They make the best strawberry tarts you've ever had."

"I'll grab one for us when I go and interview Clive." I folded the paper up, but I didn't have my handbag. But not to worry! I was a witch who had her powers back. I grinned and summoned my small, black shoulder bag. It appeared on Millicent's desk. I slid the paper inside the bag, then grabbed my phone from my back pocket to call Beren. He answered on the second ring. "Hey, will you be free this arvo to interview one of the vendors? It's Clive from Clive's Tarts in Westerham, just off High Street."

"Um, I'm a bit busy at the moment. I have tomorrow morning free if you want to organise some interviews for then. If it's only one, you should ask Imani. I know Ma'am has her working on things she can potentially drop to tail you when you're by yourself."

"Ah, okay. I can deal. I'll text you our schedule for tomorrow when I've made some of the other appointments. Can you pick me up from your aunt's? We can't just pop in and out now that we have that guest."

"Yeah, sure. Make local appointments, then. If any of the vendors have moved away, to London or further, we'll travel there, and we can leave from the PIB. Text me later, and we can chat about it tomorrow. Bye."

"Bye." I sat back in my chair and jiggled my leg up and down. As much as I wanted to just run over to Clive's and interview him, I would behave and stay put if Imani couldn't come. I dialled and crossed my fingers. "Hey, lady. Any chance you can come with me to Westerham soon. There's someone I want to interview for the Oliver Smith case. It should only take ten minutes, plus there'll be strawberry tarts."

Imani laughed. "I totally have time for that, love. When do you want to go? I can be there in fifteen."

"Maybe meet me at Ma'am's. I'm thinking we can arrive and then do a no-notice spell, sneak out the front, and pretend to come in the front door. What do you think?"

"Sounds good to me. See you there in fifteen."

I hung around in Liv's office, and before I left, she managed to track down three more vendors to go with the company purchasers. She printed off the details, and I bagged them. "Do you think you could arrange the interviews for tomorrow. Maybe make them forty minutes apart?

They all seem to be within twenty minutes' drive from each other. And I don't think we need long to ask a few questions."

"Yep, sure. I'll email you the details when I'm done." She smiled.

"You're totally the best. Thank you." I grinned. "Okay, I'm off. I'll let you know how I go at Clive's, and you can pass it on to James if there's anything interesting."

"Will do. And don't forget the pie!"

"As if I'd forget something to do with food." I rolled my eyes. "Don't you know me at all?"

She laughed. "Have fun."

"You too." I made a doorway and walked through.

CHAPTER 10

While I waited for Imani in Angelica's reception room, I called Clive and asked if he minded having a quick chat. Thankfully, he was okay with it. When Imani arrived, we snuck out without Mrs Soames hearing anything. The stupid cockatoo squawked and flapped, but as Mrs Soames had no idea why the bird was being weird, she just told it to be quiet. She likely couldn't hear us with our spell in place, plus the cockatoo, and television. For once, having the cockatoo be a noisy pain in the butt actually helped.

We walked up to High Street and turned left. Across the road a short way along was Clive's Tarts—a cute little shop in an old row of terraces with The Courtyard Café on one side and a fruit and vegetable shop on the other.

Just before we entered the tart shop, I turned to Imani. "Have you been to The Courtyard Café before?"

"Can't say I have. Want to try it next week?"

"Thanks for not making me twist your arm. It looks good." My stomach grumbled. If I wasn't planning on buying some tarts—yes, plural because if Clive had savoury ones, I was going to have some for a late lunch, and then, of course, strawberry tart for dessert—I would have grabbed something from the café. I hadn't had time to eat with all the work stuff going on, and if I was being honest, I'd admit to feeling a bit sorry for myself and my lack of opportunity to eat.

I opened the door to Clive's, and Imani followed me in. A display counter filled with delicious-looking pastries ran down the left side of the rectangular interior with four-seater tables and chairs lined up down the right side, leaving a narrow walkway in the middle. The incredible scent of freshly baked pastry infused the air, making saliva drench my mouth. Okay, that sounded gross, but could you blame my body for reacting?

A teenage girl served an old lady at the counter, and an older couple sat eating at one of the tables. A slim, middle-aged, balding man, also behind the counter, saw us and walked over to where we stood. "Can I help you, ladies?"

I smiled, wanting to appear as amiable as possible. He could very well tell me nothing if he so chose. "Hi. I'm Lily Bianchi. I spoke to you on the phone a little earlier."

He didn't return my smile but wore a guarded expression. "Aye, that I did. I'm not sure whether I can help you, lass, but tell me what you wanted to know."

Hmm, not off to the best start, but at least he hadn't

kicked us out. I couldn't really let on that it was a murder investigation because the Kent police hadn't changed their verdict on that, and now that we were involved, there wasn't going to be much information going out to the general public. The top officials in the police that knew about us would be notified of our findings, but as far as the other non-witches were concerned, Oliver had died of a drug overdose. "I'm doing a study on why people sell their homes. It's for my university degree in property." I slunk into my best sad face. "Oliver Smith was my mentor before he died, and he mentioned you'd be a good person to ask."

His nonplussed expression fell into a frown. "Ah, yes, poor Olly." He shook his head. "Sad business, that. Well, if he said I'd be a good person to ask, then I'll definitely help you. I decided to sell because my wife died, and both my kids had moved out—they're at university too, but up in London. Smart kids they are, took after their mum. Anyway, the house was too big for me. What am I going to do with five bedrooms?"

"And was that the only reason?"

He nodded. "Aye. That's reason enough, lass. Was there anything else you wanted to ask?"

I hid my disappointment at the fact that ghosts hadn't been mentioned even once. "Ah, no. thank you so much for helping me out. You'd actually be surprised that that's one of the most common answers—children moving out and the house being too big for the people, or person, who's left. Is it okay if we look at your tarts? I'm thinking I'd like to buy one."

He finally found his smile. "Aye, of course. We have savoury ones and sweet ones. Take your time."

I smiled. "Thanks." I didn't say anything to Imani while we perused the offerings, and I bought a small meat-pie for lunch, a large strawberry tart, and a chicken and leek pie for dinner, and Imani bought an apple tart. Once we were outside and headed home, I created a bubble of silence. "That wasn't the answer I was looking for."

Imani shrugged. "It's only the first person. Don't fret—maybe the others will give you a better clue tomorrow. Besides, we bought tarts. You gotta be happy about that." She grinned, her straight white teeth bright against her gorgeous dark skin. Her dimples were infectious—whenever they came out, I had to smile too, kind of like when someone yawned and created the yawning domino effect.

"If you say so. Do you think he was telling the truth?"

"Yes. I've had a lot of experience with interviewing people, even without using my magic, and he wasn't hiding anything. If you don't trust his timing, you can check out when his wife died and when his kids went off to uni."

I sighed. "There probably isn't any point unless all the others have a similar story, and we think they're hiding something. We sure could use Ma'am's mind-reading abilities."

Imani frowned. "You know that's a last-resort thing, Lily."

"Yeah, yeah, I know, but there has to be some advantage to being a witch and fighting crime. Speaking of which, have you heard anything about Will lately?"

"Sorry, no. The other agent he's paired with has been MIA too. It's probably just the case they're working." She gave me a reassuring stare. "He'll be okay. Try not to think about it."

I barked a short laugh. "Yeah, thanks for at least not patronising me and telling me not to worry."

"That would be an impossibility. I shouldn't say this, but even I'm worried." She patted my shoulder. "No matter what happens, I've got your back, Lily. I'm here for you."

Nausea washed back and forth in my stomach. For her to say that…. I sighed. Well, at least we had pie.

◈

OH, WHAT A RESTLESS SLEEP I HAD. I WOKE UP AT LEAST three times, breathing heavily, sure there was someone standing over my bed about to kill me. There was never anyone there, but still, try telling my sleep-addled brain that. Even Ethel couldn't screech loud enough to get me out of bed early. I slept until eight. Beren and my first interview wasn't until nine, so I had plenty of time to wake myself up and become presentable.

Once I'd gone to the toilet, washed my hands and face, and brushed my hair, I was awake enough to spell my PIB uniform on. It was sooooo good to have my powers back. In the future, I would be doubly careful to not risk them again, although not dying was the best excuse I could come up with. If I'd given up, I wouldn't be here to miss my magic, and even I thought that was worse.

While I ate breakfast and enjoyed my coffee, Mrs Soames joined me, Ethel perched threateningly on her shoulder. That bird had a sharp beak, and Angelica had the damaged windowsills to prove it. "Good morning, Lily. Have you gotten anywhere with the ghost research? I would really like to go home soon."

Well, at least she'd started with good morning. Besides, beating around the bush just meant an unnecessarily longer conversation, so even though it seemed abrupt, I wasn't going to complain. "Not yet, but we might have some promising leads. I'll let you know tomorrow how we're going. Believe me, I would love to see you go home too." *Tell the lady how you really feel, why don't you?* I laughed mentally—not crazily, but in my own head. Okay, so it may have been crazily too. "Um, you know what I mean."

She smirked. "I do know what you mean, but don't worry; the feeling's mutual."

"Rawrk, mutual, rawrk!"

I snorted. Yep, Mrs Soames and Ethel both knew the quickest way to get to the point, niceties be damned. Would it be too much to add that I wouldn't miss them?

The doorbell rang. Saved by the bell! There was a reason there were clichés—some situations must be acknowledged as universally experienced, and it was easier to just say the expected phrase than have to come up with one of your own—there was just no easier way to say some things. Why fix it if it ain't broke? See what I did there?

"That'll be my friend. I'm going out." I stood and put my plate and cup in the dishwasher—no magicking in front of the guest. "See you later." I left Mrs Soames to drink her tea in the esteemed, feathered company of Ethel.

As soon as I was out the door, I magicked my handbag to myself—Mrs Soames couldn't see me out here. Beren had already gotten back into the car. I got in. "Morning."

"Good morning." He smiled. "I got you a little something."

Huh? What would he—I grinned. A large takeaway coffee cup with COSTA on the side sat invitingly in one of the cupholders. I grabbed it and took the top off—foamy milk with chocolate sprinkled on the top. Mmm. I licked the lid, took a sip, and sighed. "Thank you! You're the best!" I put the lid back on and clicked in my seat belt.

"I try. Besides, I need you to remind Liv how awesome I am and how she needs to say yes to another date." He grinned.

"Oh my God! How did last night go? I totally forgot with all the crap going on in my head. Sorry."

"I'm not one to kiss and tell." He winked.

"Like that, is it? Ha!" It must have gone well. *Yay*! If my grin was any wider, it would reach my ears. "I'm so pleased. It's okay if you don't want to chat about it—I'll just get all the juicy details from Liv later." I winked.

He shook his head and laughed. "Women."

"You say that like it's a bad thing. You know you guys would have it easier if you opened up to each other. Holding all that stuff in—good and bad—is a recipe for disaster, if you ask me."

"Yeah, yeah." He pulled into the street and turned right,

heading for High Street. "Our first interview is with Mr and Mrs Benson. They're in their early thirties, no kids. They sold to one of the companies, and it only took two days to sell after their home went on the market, but we have a problem." He turned right at the main road.

"Oh, what's that?"

He glanced at me before looking back at the road. I wasn't quite sure what to make of his serious expression. "Every vendor Liv spoke with agreed to talk to us, but they also said they probably wouldn't be able to tell us much because they had to sign a nondisclosure agreement stating they wouldn't discuss any details of the sale except what is public knowledge—e.g. purchase price and how long it was on the market. Oh, and four of the vendors Liv tried to contact have died since their properties settled. They were all over the age of seventy."

"Oh, crap. That's… well… suspicious, terrible…." I blew out a huge breath and shook my head. If that wasn't strange, I didn't know what was. "Clive from the tart shop had no problem talking to us yesterday, unless he was lying, but Imani doesn't think he was. He said he'd sold because his wife had died, and his kids had left home. The house was just too big for one person. Wouldn't he have said if he'd signed a non-disclosure thingy? Everyone else told Liv."

"He's the one who sold to an individual, isn't he? And didn't he sell at the beginning of the weirdness?"

"Yes. So you're thinking his property isn't part of what-ever's going on?"

"Yep." He put his blinker on, and we turned right.

"We're almost there. The couple are renting while they look for somewhere to live." Within two minutes, we pulled up outside a two-storey, rundown block of units. The low brick front fence was leaning outwards, and a cracked concrete path to the front door denoted the midline between two halves of lawn that were mostly dirt with a sprinkling of rubbish and one old armchair. I frowned. The fact that people lived like this was depressing.

It was time to focus on why we were here, so I pushed my feelings aside. "Have you got the details of the property they sold?"

Beren turned off the car and mumbled something. A pile of paper appeared in his hand. "Here. Information on all the properties we're looking at today, plus the ones of the deceased vendors."

"You know, we could probably chat to their next of kin. They wouldn't be under the same restrictions about talking, and surely the vendors would have told them what was going on leading up to selling their house when they weren't under a binding agreement."

"That's a great idea. Hang on a sec, and I'll get Liv onto it." While Beren called Olivia, I shuffled through the papers till I found the printed web advertising for Mr and Mrs Benson's house. Woah! They'd sold a two-storey, five-bedroom stone house. The original asking price was over two-million pounds, but according to the government records, they sold for one million five hundred and twenty pounds. My mouth fell open. That was a ridiculous amount to drop in order to sell, especially when it had only been on the market for two days. When Beren finished his call, I asked, "Do we know if their asking price was reasonable, all things being equal?"

Beren took the sheet and looked it over. "Yep, that looks like what you'd expect to pay. My uncle lives near there, and he only bought two years ago. Paid a bit over two million quid for something similar."

If all the properties had dropped by a similar amount, it would mean the price drop estimates I'd read about weren't realistic—it was much worse.

Beren got out and opened my door. We walked together to the units. How far they'd fallen. But why, and would they be able to tell us? If there was ever a need for mind-reading abilities, it was now.

Just outside the door to the block, he stopped and faced me. "Lily?"

"Yes?"

"I forgot to tell you one small thing." He turned his head and looked around, then looked back at me and whispered, "I need you to spell a bubble of silence when we get inside." I opened my mouth to ask why, but Beren shook his head. "Don't ask. Right now, we're on the job, and you have to obey orders immediately, no questions asked."

I swallowed. His bossiness had taken me off guard. I wrinkled my forehead and pressed my lips together. So many questions were jostling against each other, pushing to escape the confines of my mouth, wanting to be the first out, but I had to hold them in. I grunted, which he took for an okay as he nodded and went inside the common area vestibule. I should get some kind of award for the effort that had taken.

The Bensons' rental apartment was on the ground floor. The common hallway had the original 60s vinyl floor tiles, but the paint had recently been renewed, and it seemed clean enough, which was better than the outside. Beren knocked, and I hung back, as usual. I always felt like a fake when I was out on PIB business since I wasn't an agent. But that insecurity would never be enough to make me change my mind and take up Angelica's job offer.

A broad-shouldered, dark-haired man answered the door. He was a couple of inches shorter than Beren, and while he generally looked fit, a slight paunch bulged under his dark blue jumper.

Beren said, "Hi, I'm Beren DuPree. My secretary, Olivia, spoke to you late yesterday." Mr Benson nodded and held out his hand. They shook. "This is my partner, Lily Bianchi." I held out my hand, and we did the shake thing too.

Introductions done, Mr Benson stepped out of the way and opened the door wider. "Please come in."

Beren said, "After you."

I led the way straight into what appeared to be the living room. I mumbled the bubble-of-silence spell as I took in the dated décor of brown shagpile carpet, bright turquoise walls, and dome-shaped lights that had ugly gold-painted borders all the way around. A short, slim woman I suspected was Mrs Benson stood from her place on the faux-suede couch and held her hand out. "Hi. I'm Adele Benson."

I shook her hand. "I'm Lily Bianchi. Thanks for letting us come and talk to you."

"Please have a seat." She waved at the couch, and I sat. "Can I get you anything? A cup of tea, glass of water?"

I smiled. "No thanks. I'm fine. Just had my coffee." I took my pen and notepad out of my bag—my memory could be crappy, and normally someone doing interviews had a notepad. Since Beren hadn't whipped one out, I supposed it was up to me.

Beren sat next to me, and Mrs Benson sat in an armchair that matched the couch. Mr Benson perched on the arm of the couch closest to Beren. "As I said on the phone, I'm not sure we can say a lot. We probably can't be of much help."

Beren folded his hands on his lap. "Well, we'll see how we go. I'll ask some questions, and if you can't answer them, that's okay."

"Okay," said Mr Benson. He folded his arms while Mrs Benson sat back in her armchair and folded her legs under her. Her large eyes and hunched shoulders made her look like a frightened animal. What was the price of breaking their agreement?

Beren started the interview. "What made you choose Smith & Henderson to sell your house?"

The tightness around Mr Benson's eyes relaxed. "Around the time we decided to sell, we found their brochure in our letterbox."

"Do you remember if the brochure appeared before or after you decided to sell?"

The couple looked at each other, and Mrs Benson said, "Just before." As soon as she finished talking, her hand flew to her mouth, and she chewed her fingernail. What had she left out? It was as if there was more to say, but she'd restrained herself.

"Was there something else you wanted to say?" I couldn't help interrupting. Hopefully I wasn't messing with Beren's interview plan, if he even had one.

She shook her head emphatically. I turned to Beren and shrugged. It was his turn to ask a question.

"Why did you want to sell?"

Mr Benson shrugged and coughed. "We wanted a change." His fake smile was such an obvious tell, but there was nothing we could do about it. These people had done nothing wrong, and this was an interview, not an interrogation. It seemed like we had to guess which questions were off limits, not that it was hard.

Beren nodded. "Fair enough. Was there a reason you took a lot less than what you were originally asking?"

Mrs Benson choked—maybe her nail went down the wrong way. She stood and rasped, "Excuse me. I need a glass of water." She hurried to the kitchen, which was through an arched doorway with no door. The fridge facing the opening was visible from where I sat.

Mr Benson shrugged. "I guess we realised we'd gone in too high, and we didn't want the property to sit around for months because that would hurt our chances of selling. It's quite a competitive market, you know."

"But Oliver was one of the best agents in the area.

Surely he advised you of what price to sell it at in the first place?" Beren was asking the hard questions, all right. He wasn't actually getting honest answers though.

Was that sweat popping up on Mr Benson's brow? "Ah, well, um…." He took his jumper off to reveal a white T-shirt with faded writing that said Sorry I'm Late, But I Was Walking My Corgi.

It was up to me to ask the obvious questions, but he could probably answer this, as I doubted it would have been anything whoever wrote the non-disclosure agreement would have foreseen as a problem. "Do you have any pets, Mr Benson?"

His shoulders sagged. "No. We had two corgis, but this is a pet-free rental, so we had to find them new homes. We're hoping to get them back when we get into a house. We just needed to save money while we look for something else." He snapped his mouth shut, probably thinking he'd said too much.

"Did you have a mortgage on your house?" Even though they'd sold for well under what they wanted, their selling price was still pretty hefty.

"Yes, we did. Look, this is getting rather personal. I can't answer any more questions. Sorry. I think we've helped you all we can." He stood and walked to the front door.

Mrs Benson, obviously hearing we were leaving, came to the kitchen opening. "Thanks for coming by. Sorry we couldn't be of more help."

Beren and I stood. How disappointing. We hadn't gotten nearly enough information. As we walked to the door, I flung out a question that would hopefully take them off guard. "Do you believe in ghosts?"

Mr Benson blinked, his eyes wide, and his wife paled. No one said a word until Mr Benson opened the door and found his voice. "Drive safely." I was going to take that as a yes. If they wanted to keep their secrets secret, they needed to take Ma'am's poker-face 101 class. She really should run those, although they likely already had those classes for agents. I probably needed to take one too.

Once we were back in the car, Beren created a bubble of silence. "No clear answers, but I'm pretty sure they still told us more than they wanted to. Nice curveball at the end, Lily."

I smiled. "Why, thank you. I like to be unpredictable." Okay, so most of the PIB crew wouldn't say that was actually something to be proud of, but it had served me well so far.

"The next person we're going to see is a forty-year-old lady—Miranda Thomas. She's an ambulance officer."

I picked through the papers and found the ones pertaining to her sale. She'd sold her two-bedroom apartment for 50,000 less than what she paid two years earlier. Yikes. Nice apartment, by the looks of things. The real-estate photos showed polished parquetry floors, kitchen with stone benchtops, and it even had views over the countryside. "It says here she'd just finished renovating." Dread spilled from my shoulders and throat down to my stomach. I didn't even know this woman, but I wanted to cry. All those hours she worked doing such a stressful job, and somehow she'd been forced to sell for less than what was fair. I could only imagine how she felt right now. We didn't have definitive proof, but someone, or a group of someones, was behind this. There was no way I'd quit until we figured this out. "Supposing we do solve this one, is it likely we can get people their properties back?"

"I really don't know, but I don't like our chances. Even if we uncover some kind of plot to fleece these people, whoever owns the properties now could transfer ownership to an entity we can't touch. Or they could sell and move the money. Try not to worry about that yet—we've got a long way to go before we even solve this." Beren's sober tone didn't give me hope, and his words weren't that great either. I sighed.

As Beren pulled up outside a small bungalow, thunder rumbled from not too far away. There was a small patch of blue above us, but black clouds darkened the sky only a mile or so away. It would probably be pouring by the time we finished here. At least this cottage was cute and well-cared-for. The knee-height white picket fence was straight and immaculate. Pruned box hedges butted against the neat home. "Is she renting?"

Beren unclipped his seat belt and looked at me. "She's moved back in with her parents until she finds something else." As sad as that sounded, at least she had parents to move back in with. I didn't want to slip down the poor-me slide, but I couldn't help wondering where my parents were, or where their bodies were. All those years that had been stolen from us. I'd give my unit up in a heartbeat if I could have them back. I blinked to erase the thin veneer of moisture that welled in my eyes. Beren frowned. "Are you okay?"

"Yeah, just thinking about my parents. Sorry."

"Sorry? Don't be ridiculous. You've been through hell, and you have every right to be sad about it. Don't ever apologise for that. Do you hear me?"

I gave him a small smile. "Thanks for caring. You're a big sweetie, and I appreciate it."

"I do what I can." He winked and grinned. "Okay, let's get this done. And same as before, I'll get you to do the spell. We can't risk whoever instigated this finding out what we're doing or what those people are telling us."

"I get it. Lead the way, Agent DuPree."

A short, white-haired, rotund lady in a floral, long-sleeved loose dress and sheepskin slippers opened the door. I was guessing this was the victim's mother. She smiled. "Welcome! You must be Beren DuPree. Please come in."

"Thanks, Mrs Thomas. This is my associate, Lily Bianchi."

Beren was waiting for me to go first—always the gentleman—so I stepped inside and smiled. "Lovely to meet you, Mrs Thomas. Thanks for seeing us on short notice."

"Lovely to meet you too, Lily. What a sweet name."

My cheeks warmed slightly—I wasn't good with compliments. "Thank you." I automatically wanted to give her one back, but commenting on her name would be ridiculous. What wonderful thing could you say about Mrs Thomas? Maybe I could tell her what a happy dress she had on, but before I opened my mouth, she'd already shut the front door and was leading us down the hallway. Moment lost.

We entered a cosy sitting room that had a fire blazing in the small fireplace. I created a bubble of silence while Mrs Thomas gave a nod to another woman. "This is my daughter, Miranda. This is Beren and Lily."

Miranda, who was about my height and looked more like mid-thirties than forty with her long, wavy dark hair and bright-blue eyes, smiled. She held her hand out and shook mine vigorously. "Lovely to meet you, Lily. And Beren." She shook his hand too. Her enthusiastic tone of voice was unexpected. "Please sit down. I'll try and answer what I can, but that stupid agreement will stop me actually telling you very much. I'm terribly sorry about that."

Again, Beren and I sat next to each other on the couch —this time it was a fawn colour with tiny pink rose motifs all over it. Mrs Thomas sat on the two-seater lounge next to her daughter.

Beren smiled. "Thanks so much for talking to us on short notice. I understand if you can't tell us too much. I might start with an easy question that I hope is okay. Did you enjoy living in your unit?"

She smiled. "Yes. I loved my unit. It took me months to find one I really wanted that I could afford, so when I finally closed on that one, it was one of the happiest moments of my life." She got ten points for smiling through this disaster. I'm sure I'd be bitter as hell.

"Great. So, why did you decide to sell?"

She shrugged. "Next question." Well, that was no surprise.

"Did you ever meet the person, or people, who bought your unit?"

"No." Her smile had vanished, and her face was set in what appeared to be concentration. She must be trying hard to not say anything she wasn't supposed to. If she was someone who got carried away and blurted things out, that would be super hard—trust me, I knew all about it.

Hang on a minute. I sat forward and looked at her mother. "Mrs Thomas, are you bound by the non-disclosure agreement?"

Her face registered surprise before she gave me a sly smile and nodded. "Very clever, Lily. In fact, I'm not bound by any such agreement." Her smile deflated with her shoulders. "Oh, but I probably can't answer any questions that would help, since I can only talk about what my daughter has told me."

"No, no, that's fine. We're actually quite interested in events leading up to the sale. Miranda obviously loved her apartment, so why was she in such a hurry to sell?"

Miranda's eyes widened. "Mum, you can't say anything."

She turned to look at her daughter and placed her hands on her waist, bumping Miranda with her arm in the process. "Look, I didn't sign that agreement, so they can't do anything. You haven't told me anything, so I'm free to speak about what happened before you agreed to sell, am I not?" Wow, whatever the agreement stipulated as punishment must have been harsh to scare everyone so much. First the Bensons, and now Miranda.

Miranda looked at the ground, defeated by her mother's stare. "Okay, Mum." Gah, parents making you feel like you were ten again. I could relate to that, except the chastiser wasn't my mother—it was Angelica.

I put on my most sympathetic expression and softened my tone. "It's okay, Miranda. Your mother definitely isn't bound by the agreement you signed, and I won't ask her anything about the specifics of the sale. Okay?"

She looked up at me and nodded. She bit her lip and wrinkled her brow, maybe wondering if I was telling the truth. I looked back at Mrs Thomas. "Why did Miranda decide to put the unit on the market?"

"Well, this is going to sound out there. Please don't laugh."

I had a feeling I knew what was coming, and it was about time. I shook my head. "Definitely not. We have our suspicions anyway. We just need someone to confirm them for us."

She swallowed. "About two weeks before she decided to sell, Miranda came to me and said there was a ghost in her place. I didn't believe her, of course, until I went over there." She put a hand to her heart. "I swear on my mother's grave that her apartment was haunted. A terrible, evil apparition of a violent man. He was screaming. And he had a knife sticking out of his chest. It scared us both half to death. We tried smudge sticks and even called a priest, but nothing worked." She shook her head. "She had no choice but to sell. I don't know how anyone could live in there though. Terrifying, really. Poor Miranda had to come live with us after one week. After the second week, she decided to get rid of her place. It really was heartbreaking to watch, and to lose all that money." She grabbed her daughter's hand in both of hers. "Oh, darling, I'm so sorry. Maybe these kind investigators can help. Even if it's too late for you, maybe they can stop it from happening to someone else."

Miranda shook her head. "But how?" She looked at Beren. "Are you like Ghostbusters or something? Because if you're not, I fail to see how you can help. I mean, we can only assume I'm not the only one this has happened to; otherwise you wouldn't be here asking questions."

I nodded. "Yes, we're following a trail of suspicious property sales. I don't want to get your hopes up, but if there's any way we can make this right and get your property back to you, we will."

Beren scowled at me and hissed, "Shh, we can't make those kinds of promises."

"I haven't promised, but I will promise to try and do everything humanly"—*witchily*—"possible to help." If there was one thing I'd never back down from, it was a fight for justice.

Beren looked at Mrs Thomas. "I'm pretty sure your daughter can't answer this question, so I'll ask you, just in case she mentioned something before an agreement was reached. How did she choose an agent? Did she look a few up and ask for quotes?"

"Oh, I can answer that. We were going to do it that way,

and in fact, my husband and I were going to help her, but before we needed to, she got an advertising brochure from Smith & Henderson. We found it when we collected her mail—when she's on shift work as an ambulance officer, she doesn't have time to pass by and grab the mail from her letterbox, so we did it for her. When we called, they put us through to Oliver. He was extremely helpful, to be honest." Hmm, one thing was becoming clear: Oliver was always there when you needed him. Coincidence? Ha!

This investigation was about what had occurred, but depending on what happened to these victims in the future, maybe knowing what they were facing would help find a motive. "Are you looking for somewhere to buy at the moment?" I asked.

Miranda looked at me. "I started looking, but there's nothing for sale in my price range in the areas I want. I'm going to have to look in places maybe ten miles or so away from my old place, and even that might be difficult. I rang a couple of agents last week, and they said they'd get back to me when they had something suitable, but I haven't heard back." She sighed and slumped back in her chair.

"I know it's little consolation," her mum said, "but you can stay here as long as you need to."

She gave her mum a smile. "I know. Thanks. But it might be a lot longer than we'll both enjoy." She laughed. "It's okay. We'll figure it out, I suppose."

"That's the spirit." Her mum smiled.

They sure were dealing with this as well as could be expected. The word "spirit" made me think about the ghosts, and I shuddered. Where were they all coming from? Was some portal to hell open or something? If that was the case, total disaster couldn't be far away. Was there even a door to hell? If Angelica didn't even believe in ghosts—or didn't believe in them before Mrs Soames's ghost—then she mustn't have heard any rumours of openings to the shady underworld. Maybe we should talk to a priest sooner rather than later. If anyone would know about that stuff, it was one of those.

Beren stood. "Thanks for your time today. Sorry if it was difficult for you, Miranda, but I assure you, your mother's help won't break any agreement you've signed."

Miranda nodded. "Okay." She stood. "Let me know if you figure out what's going on. If there's any chance of getting my place back empty of ghosts, I would jump at it."

Beren smiled. "We will. And thanks to you too, Mrs Thomas."

She stood. "My pleasure."

Mrs Thomas led the way to the front door, where we all said goodbye again. Once we were in the car, I took out my notepad and wrote everything down. I'd been so engrossed in the conversation before that I'd forgotten to write at all. Yep, I was an idiot on occasion. Okay, so Angelica would probably have something snarky to say about that, but I was going with my own opinion, thank you very much.

Beren made a bubble of silence. "So, that was productive."

"It most certainly was. Looks like it's easy interviewing those close to the seller, rather than the actual seller.

Whoever set this up is pretty stupid for not thinking of that."

"Well, they're not as stupid as we'd like—they've managed to get away with this for at least three months. And that's just here. How many other places have they been operating in?"

Damn, I hadn't thought of that. I clicked my seat belt in. "How many more interviews for today?"

"Two." He pulled out his phone. "I've had this on silent, but it looks like Liv's messaged. One of the sellers who's since died has a niece who's happy to talk to us. Liv's booked it in for our last appointment."

"Right. We should get moving. It's going to be a long day."

Beren looked at me and smiled. "As long as it's productive, I don't mind." He turned the car on and pulled into the street while I crossed my fingers that we'd be a lot closer to catching the bad guys when we were done.

Unfortunately, I mustn't have crossed my fingers hard enough.

CHAPTER 11

We arrived at the PIB reception room at 3:30 p.m. "I need to eat, B. I'm starving."

He laughed. "I'm surprised you lasted that long, considering we ate lunch over three hours ago."

The door clicked open, revealing Gus the security guy. "Hello, Agent DuPree, Lily." He tipped his cap.

"Hey, Gus," I said.

"Hey, man. Great to see you. How's the missus?" Beren asked and followed me out. I was eager to hurry ahead and avoid whatever gross conversation Gus managed to produce, but James stood in the hallway, his poker face not quite in situ—traces of anger vibrated beneath it in his bunched jaw muscles and hard stare. Crap, had I done something wrong?

"Lily, Agent DuPree, please come with me. I've called an urgent meeting in the conference room." Without another word, he turned and strode away. Beren and I both gave each other confused looks, then jogged to catch up, and it didn't escape my notice that DuPree rhymed with me. I didn't dare giggle though because my brother definitely didn't look to be in the mood.

We entered the conference room on James's heels, and Beren shut the door. Ma'am, Liv, and Imani were already sitting at the large table. Imani and Liv gave Beren and I small "hello" smiles, and Liv shrugged, obviously trying to tell us that she had no idea what was going on either.

Once Beren and I sat, Ma'am started. "We've called this urgent meeting because of a tragedy."

I sucked in a breath as my stomach dropped to the floor. *Please don't tell me Will's dead. Oh God, please don't.* Angelica stared at me. "Are you all right, dear?"

I cleared my throat in an effort to find my voice. "What's the tragedy?"

She gently closed and opened her eyes in an "ah huh" moment. "We haven't heard anything from Will. This isn't about him, so you can breathe again." Which is exactly what I did while pretending I hadn't just been about to cry. "Right, team, we have a problem, a colossal one. Olivia has set up five interviews with sellers of those properties for tomorrow, and one interview with the son of one of the deceased sellers. I'm afraid to say that they've all died."

My mouth dropped open. Had she just said what I thought she'd said? Imani shared a shocked look with me before asking, "Excuse me, Ma'am, but did you just say *all* those people died? As in died today?"

"Yes. I'm afraid so. We received notification of the deaths from an anonymous source before the police were aware. It's clear they didn't just die but were killed, and it's obvious why they were killed. The murders *look* like natural deaths and two suicides. The message we received appeared on my laptop screen when I turned it on this afternoon. As soon as I read it, it disappeared. Anyone we make appointments to speak with is to be killed. We are to stop investigating this immediately." She sat up straighter and sniffed. She wasn't calling this whole thing off, was she? We had to stop these crazy murderers. This was madness! Ma'am hooked me with her glare. "Of course we're not going to pull the plug on the investigation, Lily. And no, I didn't read your mind—you have no game face." She rolled her eyes. "We really need to work on that."

My cheeks heated. Well, it wouldn't be the first time they'd gone against what I thought was the proper thing to do. But the way Ma'am was staring at me, with an "honestly" expression, I wasn't going to say a word. You had to pick your battles, and this one wasn't worth it. At least they were going to keep investigating—that was the main thing.

Angelica stood. "I'm sorry, but I have another meeting to attend. I'll leave you in Agent Bianchi's capable hands. We've discussed how to move forward, and I'm counting on you. So do your best." She made a doorway and disappeared.

James cleared his throat and was about to speak when I put up my hand. "Yes, Lily?"

"What about the people we've already spoken to? Are

they safe?" My stomach twisted with worry. They had all been lovely people, had already been through enough. This was horrific. I wouldn't know what I'd do if I found out I helped get them killed, especially after reassuring Mrs Thomas she was doing the right thing.

"We've put magical protections around their houses, stopping any witches or their magic from entering. The other victims were all killed at home. We're tailing all the people you interviewed as well. This is consuming a lot of our resources—resources we can ill afford to sacrifice. Even if we could employ more agents, we haven't got the time to train them for immediate deployment. If we have any other major incidents, we're screwed."

Oh. That was kind of shocking. My brother hardly ever swore, and I think that was the first time I'd ever heard him say "screwed." I hoped he and Angelica had put a good plan into place because this wasn't going to be easy.

James turned his gaze on Beren. "Beren, can you give me a rundown of what happened today."

"Certainly. We've deduced that all the owners sold in a hurry and for way less than what they should have gotten. We've had haunting confirmed by three sources because their close family members were present and unrestricted by the agreements the sellers had signed. We weren't privy to what the penalties for breaching the agreements were, but they must be serious because all the victims were terrified to say the wrong thing. My deduction would be that a witch, or group of witches, is haunting these houses and forcing the people to sell. I would imagine the agent who died, Oliver, was under instructions to make sure the vendors sold to those companies—regardless of how low the purchase price was. If they were operating under normal circumstances, he would have received less per sale because agents work on commission—the higher the sale price, the better. But since he had to do so little legwork to sell them, maybe he thought it was acceptable." Beren magicked a glass of water into his hand and took a sip. "In any case, the motive appears to be cheap property; however, there must be more to this because the perpetrators have gone to extreme lengths to stop people from talking, and they're only targeting non-witches." Would this all stop now Oliver was dead, or would another agent take up the slack? Samuel, maybe?

"Like an ethnic cleansing?" I asked. I mean, it seemed as if they'd forced all these non-witches out. Obviously selling in a hurry, they were still having problems trying to find somewhere to live. Making them take less than expected prices sounded like something you'd do to someone you hated—we weren't just talking walking away with a good deal, here. Some of the amounts were life-changing in a negative way.

James looked at me. "I'm sorry to say that your estimation seems to fit. So, what are we going to do about it?"

I frowned. "I thought that's what *you* were going to tell *us*."

He raised an eyebrow. "It was a rhetorical question. Of course I'm going to tell you what we're going to do. We can't interview anyone or be seen investigating the murders, but we're still digging into who owns the companies that bought the houses. We've set up a few computers on a different system. Olivia has access to one. We can find most of what we need that way. I also have a friend in local government who can help if we're desperate. We're also investigating the people living there now, who all happen to be witches, so your theory is likely correct, Lily." I smiled, quite proud of myself. They were rare moments when I was being praised rather than chastised, so I enjoyed it when it happened. "We need to establish if these people are in on it or not. The other thing we need to do is stop this from happening while we get to the bottom of it. Which means we're going to have to figure out how these witches are managing to put ghosts in peoples' houses, or if, in fact, they're magicking the whole scenario."

Olivia sat forward. "Are you saying the ghosts aren't even real?"

"Maybe not."

"But what about the one I saw in Mrs Soames's place? It even moved things and tried to kill us! If that was a witch magicking the ghost, wouldn't it mean they were spying on us as they did it? Otherwise, how would they know what we were saying and where we were standing?"

Beren looked at me. "Surveillance video. It would be easy for them to break in, install stuff, and leave without anyone realising they'd been there." Of course it would, and I should've thought of that already.

James nodded at me. "This is where you can help, Lily. Are you still getting those photography jobs?"

"Yes. I've got four for tomorrow. Today was a day off because of Oliver's death. The office is having a day for his funeral."

"Right, well, I need you to ask your magic to show you the surveillance cameras and who put them in. Even if the witches weren't there to install the actual cameras, they would have had to have been inside at some point to visualise exactly where they were going to put them. We should be able to sneak you into the murder scenes too. Even though Oliver was killed somewhere else and magicked into his office, maybe these victims weren't. We've also got a tail on the guy who took over—Samuel. If there's any way to stop the hauntings and stop people from selling, we need to make it happen. And ultimately, we want to find these bastards and put them in jail, where they belong." Amen to that. But it wasn't so simple.

"If whoever's doing this has watched us go and do interviews, they'll know I'm working with you. Won't they start killing people if they see me at one of the houses? And wouldn't they tell Samuel not to use me?" This was an issue. And since witches could see through any magical disguise because of the orange thing, that was a no go either.

James wrinkled his brow. "I don't know. They might, but they don't know about your talent. Maybe they'll just keep a close eye on you? You can still do what you need to if someone's in the room, can't you?"

"Yeah. I can ask my magic in my mind. It doesn't have

to come out of my mouth, and it's not like anything happens when I take a photo. It's business as usual, but still, we don't want to provoke them."

James sat back in his chair. "Hmm…. Has Samuel cancelled your appointments yet?"

I shook my head. "Not that I know of. Hang on, and I'll check my emails." I got my phone out of my bag and went to the mail app. "Nope. Nothing."

"Well, I say you go as per normal; just be careful."

"But what if they kill more people?"

Beren looked at me. "I don't think they will, Lily. It's clear they have the upper hand, and if they trust Samuel, they probably aren't monitoring the advertising stuff since it's just a formality, and they likely have no idea that you're the one taking the photos. We could bleach your hair and give you a pair of glasses so that anyone watching from a distance doesn't immediately recognise you?"

"I suppose that could work. But me as a blonde? I'm not so sure about that." I snorted. It was stupid of me to even be thinking of that, but if they couldn't get me back to brown easily afterwards, I was going to be stuck with it for a while. Maybe I could borrow one of the PIB wigs?

"You'll look gorgeous for sure," said Olivia.

"I'm not convinced this is going to work, but we have to try, I suppose." There didn't seem to be any other way, so this was it.

"Good," said James. "While you're gathering as much evidence as you can, Lily, I'll have another couple of agents acting on the information Olivia unearths. Beren can sit tight, as I'll need him for a different investigation we're in the middle of, and Imani can shadow you, Lily, as per usual. How does that sound?"

"Sounds good," said Beren.

Imani and I nodded, and Liv said, "Yep, all good."

James stood. "Let's get to it!"

CHAPTER 12

There were forty-five minutes to go before my first real-estate job of the day, but I stood frozen in front of the mirror, unable to decide whether I should leave the house. Okay, maybe it was an overreaction, but, oh my God, my blonde hair did not suit my winter-paled olive complexion. It was official: I looked sick, and not the teenage version of sick—meaning smoking hot. I looked as if I needed to get back to bed and take some vitamins. The large round frames of my new glasses were bright purple. At least people would be too shocked by my white-and-purple brightness to even notice what my features looked like.

I took a deep breath. "Get it together, woman. What you look like doesn't matter." And it didn't. I took my advice and snuck downstairs to grab breakfast before I left—I didn't want Mrs Soames to hear me and bother me while I ate. Yeah, that was pretty crummy, but we had nothing in common, and I was always waiting for her to get angry or annoyed about something and whinge to me, which was not a pleasant way to wake up.

An interesting idea came while I sipped my coffee, uninterrupted, thank God. If there weren't actually any ghosts—which hadn't been proven yet, but we'd see—I could probably test the theory in Mrs Soames's place. Maybe we could do a spell that froze the recordings or transmission of data through the cameras; then I could go in without the bad witches knowing, and if there was no ghost, the theory would just about be proven. If it worked, we could get Mrs Soames back into her house sooner rather than later. That would be awesome. It would also mean we could start clearing other houses before they sold.

I crossed my fingers. If all went as I planned, it would work. But that sounded too easy, and when was anything I ever did without its disasters and problems? I pushed my purple glasses up my nose, case in point. After grabbing my equipment, I slid into the car. My first job had been changed to a home about fourteen miles from here rather than one in Westerham itself. Samuel had emailed me last night at 10:00 p.m. Apparently it was urgent because it was an expensive house, and Samuel wanted to make sure the clients felt looked after. Maybe this wasn't going to be one of those haunted houses, and he had to work to earn the sale?

The journey was pleasant enough, if not slower than I'd like with morning traffic, but I pulled up to the property just on time. I ignored the nerves zipping around my belly warning that something bad might happen to the people we'd interviewed if I showed up to this job. Samuel was a non-witch, though. Maybe the witch criminals hadn't told him exactly who they were or what they were doing? I could hope.

Rather than drive up to the parking area and get in the way of any long-range shots, I pulled to the side of the wide gravel driveway behind another parked car. I *could* edit that stuff out, but better to start without it if possible. We were still around one hundred metres from the home, an expanse of lawn and gravel parking area between us.

I cut the engine and got out. Samuel hopped out of the car in front of me. "Morning. Can I help you?"

"Hi, Samuel. It's me, Lily." Okay, so the disguise worked. That was a hell of a lot easier than I thought it would be. But still, he knew who I was now that I'd told him, and if the bad guys had said anything to him, I could still be in danger. But maybe they hadn't said anything to him about them being witches and our investigation, and if they were spying right now, they wouldn't know I was me. And that made total sense. My life was beyond confusing these days.

He laughed. "Oh, I didn't recognise you, obviously. You've changed a few things?"

Typical man couldn't figure out what was different. I resisted an eye-roll. "Um, just a couple. Anyway, where would you like to start? This is an amazing property." And that was an understatement. Sprawled in front of us was a double-storey, rendered-brick, white Regency mansion that went on forever—I counted eight chimneys on its grey roof. On over seven acres, it really was more of an estate than just a home.

"Yes. This one's going to take a couple of hours, I'd imagine. I've moved our other appointments to later in the day. I hope that's all right."

"Yes, that's fine. I had nothing on this afternoon." I smiled. I'd be working late to get these edited and sent back by tomorrow, but maybe I could use my magic to do it quicker. Hmm, why had I never thought of that before? Probably because I didn't mind the creative process, and, to be honest, I'd had time lately. It was just now things were getting busy again.

Samuel handed me a shot list—which had a roughly sketched floor plan attached—and explained all the shots he wanted. I took a quick look and shoved it in my pocket. The first shot was obviously a wide one, which encompassed that grandness upon first seeing it. I started by setting up my tripod on the grass. The pics I took showed the magnificent size of the home in its expansive setting with the sweeping circular driveway that passed the grand entrance door. Once that was done, we hopped in our cars and drove to the parking area so I wouldn't have to lug my heavy equipment too far.

After I'd dragged my equipment out of the car for the second time, a forceful, chilly gust swept past, flapping the bottom of my coat and making me shiver. I looked up. The sky was mostly blue with only a few wispy white clouds hanging around. And whilst it was cold, the air was fairly still… except for that shot of breeze. Another car came along the driveway towards us, kicking up dust that hovered in place before settling again. Yep, no wind. So what had that chill been all about?

"Ah, the copywriter's here." Samuel turned to me. "The front door's open. Why don't you get the entry shots while I get our writer organised? When you're done with the entry, move around as you need to. This one has a large budget, so go to town. Get us shots of every room, as per the list I gave you, and I'll choose later."

"Sounds good to me. Just out of interest, how many bedrooms does this place have?"

"Eleven." His close-mouthed smile was a bit sharkish, and I was anticipating him rubbing his hands together in glee any moment. Maybe he was seeing commission dollar signs—or pound signs—in the air.

"Wow, okay. I'll see you inside soon."

A small stone-paved porch led to two four-paned windows that sat to either side of the massive arched timber front door, matching coach lights nestled between window and door frames. The door was ajar, so I nudged it open enough to fit myself through, in case they had the heating on. When I stepped inside, I pouted. It was just as cold in here as outside. My fingers and nose were suffering, and the blood supply to those areas appeared to be on strike. I should have worn gloves. Should I magic myself some? Hmm, probably not. If the witches who'd cooked up the whole ripping-people-off scheme were around, they'd feel my magic. I did not need to draw attention to myself. I would have to suffer in silence, so I might as well get this done as quickly as possible, which was a shame since I loved old buildings.

I set the camera on top of the tripod and took a few pictures of the entry and turned-timber staircase, with its thick dark timber bannister and stair treads. A Persian stair runner in blue and white led upstairs and was held in place against each stair-back by a gold rod—swanky. I sent my thought to the universe. *Show me a witch installing video cameras.* Halfway up the stairs, on the landing, a man in a pastel-blue jumper stood with his back to me. *Yes!* This meant the ghosts weren't real; at least I thought it meant that. The witches needed the cameras to spy on their victims so they could interact in real time. The only other alternative was that they'd managed to control ghosts, which would be pretty impossible. There were so many ghost stories floating around—pardon the pun—but in none of them were ghosts ever controlled by anyone. Unless they'd talked all the ghosts into taking over these homes? *Argh, stop thinking!* My brain was making life harder for me, yet again. I needed to find an assumption and stick with it.

I took a deep breath and focussed on the vision through the lens. The man's head was tilted back, towards me, while he gazed at the corner three-quarters of the way up the wall. *Click.* He seemed to be staring at a small, round, black device, but when I looked at the wall without my Nikon, there was nothing there. Could they have made all the devices invisible, and if they had, how the hell was I supposed to check it out?

Muffled voices chatting came from the other side of the front door; then it opened. I straightened from looking through the viewfinder and turned. Samuel held the door open for another man in a white suit, black shirt, and no tie. He was around forty, and had wavy dark hair, chocolate-brown eyes, and a goatee. He was a smidge taller than Samuel, of average build, and fairly attractive. Nevertheless, my hackles rose. Samuel followed him in and shut the door.

Click.

I looked at the guy with my other sight and quickly manifested a return-to-sender spell. Yep, he was a witch. I didn't want to overreact, but he gave me the creeps. I mean who wore a white suit around except a man who was overly confident or part of the Mafia?

"Lily, this is Adrian, our copywriter." Yep, double creeps. All the other copywriters I'd met had dressed neatly but still fairly casual. This guy was over the top.

"Pleased to meet you." His accent was Eastern European and his grin way too smooth, as if he thought he was God's gift to women. Not this woman, buddy. He held his hand out. I didn't want to shake it, but if I didn't, I'd look rude, and the guy who had the power to give me more work was standing right there. This could be his best friend, for all I knew.

"Lovely to meet you too," I lied and shook his clammy hand. He tried to hold on for over three seconds, but I was having none of it. I snatched my hand away. "I have to get to work. This house won't photograph itself." I gave a nervous laugh. He was probably harmless, but that didn't mean I had to leave my hand in his for longer than was absolutely necessary. I also hoped he'd washed his hands last time he went to the toilet. Hmm, maybe I'd wash my hands at the end of this job because there was no way I was touching my lunch with that hand, just in case.

He looked at Samuel. "And I shall get started too." He pulled out a notebook and pen and wandered through one of the two doorways leading off the vestibule. Just because he was a witch, didn't mean he couldn't be a copywriter. I was a photographer doing this, after all.

I went through the doorway on my left and set my tripod up in the next room, which happened to be the games room. Ornate cornices in a crenellated pattern bordered lofty ceilings. Chestnut-coloured parquetry floors sat underneath a billiard table, and a massive timber fireplace sat mid-wall to my right. To my left, tall double timber-and-glass doors opened to the side garden. Light streamed in. This room was the epitome of wealth and the good life. I could easily live here. Shame I needed over three million quid to do it. Ah, the things I'd learnt from my latest research.

I turned my camera on again and sniffed the chilly air. The scent of old smoke permeated the room, and ash coated the bottom of the fireplace. You'd think they would have lit a fire for the shoot. That would have lent the photos a gorgeous and cosy atmosphere. Maybe I should suggest it? Or maybe they didn't care because they already had a buyer? I guessed it wouldn't matter if this was all just a set up to get the owner over the line and not report them to anyone for dodgy service, plus the owners paid for all this out of their own pockets. My mouth dropped open. The agent would make money on that too because didn't everyone build a profit into offered services?

Guilt dampened my enthusiasm for the home. I was taking people's money, money they shouldn't even be spending. But then again, maybe the universe had sent me here to solve the crime and stop this from happening to lots of other people. Besides, they would have paid someone else to do it if it wasn't me. Still, I didn't have to be happy about it. But would I return the money? Probably not, not that I received much of it. The copywriter and floor-plan person got their share, then add in the agent's cut. Still, the right thing to do would be to return my fees to each of the affected parties. I could afford it, so I probably should. I sighed. Who was I kidding? Of course I was going to return the money to the individual owners. Being a decent person was often quite painful.

After photographing for the ad, I whispered, "Show me the witch installing the hidden cameras." No one was in the room, so I figured it was safe to say it if I was super quiet. I took my camera off the tripod and peered through the lens. And there the guy in blue was again, back to me, hands in the air, palms pointing to a black camera sitting in a nook where the cornice met the wall above the fireplace. *Click.*

I packed up and went through a door to the next room —the sitting room. It smelled like leather polish with the faint hint of smoke. This room also had the rich-aristocrat vibe with parquetry floors, ornately carved timber fireplace with a gilt-framed mirror hanging above it, two Chesterfields, and a grand piano with expensive knickknacks on it.

So far, I was getting some evidence to support our theory, which was great, but was it enough? I hadn't even seen the witch's face who was installing these cameras. I'd have to ask for that specifically.

Once again, I photographed the room first, then grabbed my camera off the tripod. *Show me the face of the witch installing the cameras.*

Oh, crap.

I hadn't recognised him from behind in the previous photos, but the guy in the blue jumper was the copywriter. Goosebumps peppered my arms. Was I safe in here?

My phone rang, and I jumped. I rolled my eyes at myself as I put my camera on the coffee table; then I slid my phone out of my back pocket. Imani's name was on the screen. "Hey. Good time for you to call." At least I could tell her what was going on.

Her tone was urgent. "Lily, I have some—"

Huh? She had some what? Chocolate, coffee, news? "Hello? Are you there? Hello?" I checked the bars on my phone—I had three. I put it to my ear again. Nothing. I tried to call her back, but it went to voicemail.

Grr, stupid phones. I looked around, making sure I was safe. Everything looked as it had before. Maybe she wanted to see how I was going? Or maybe Liv had unearthed some new information. Whatever it was, it would have to wait until I was done with this job. To that end, I made my way through fantabulous room after fantabulous room. If I ever managed to make oodles of money, this was how I'd live—surrounded by antique furniture, fireplaces, and elegance. Although, one day, I'd certainly be able to afford at least a nice one- or two-bedroom flat that I could furnish nicely. I'd just make sure it had a fireplace and high ceilings. It was really the feel of the place I was after—what would one person do in a mega mansion like this? It would probably feel lonely after a while, plus I'd have to be rich enough to afford a cleaner because it would be a full-time job dealing with this place.

Eventually I made it to the first of five bathrooms upstairs, which was warmer than the rest of the house. The large rectangular room was as big as my bedroom. A double-bowl timber vanity stood against the wall to my right, and a claw-footed bath placed in the centre of the room drew the eye. Someone had filled it with water, and a handful of lilies floated on the top. I'd have to check if they were plastic because I had to know. It was one of those weird things, like touching an indoor plant to see if it was real or not.

A frameless glass shower with two shower heads nestled in the far-right corner, and the old-style toilet, against the wall to my left, had one of those high, wall-mounted cisterns with the pull chain. The floor was wide timber boards. Wouldn't it swell when wet? Who knew? Maybe rich people didn't care about stuff like that because they could just get it repaired. If you were a witch, you could fix it with magic, so

I supposed as far as I was concerned, it wouldn't be a problem. I laughed. I could only afford an apartment slightly bigger than this bathroom, so chances were, I'd have to live in this area. I guessed a single mattress would fit.

The only thing that spoiled the look of the whole thing was a small electric heater sitting near the bath, humming away, which was obviously the reason this room wasn't so cold. I placed my tripod just to the left of the doorway and set my bag down outside in the hallway. Then I went to unplug the heater and move it out of the way so it wouldn't ruin the shot. Just before I bent down, a voice said, "There you are." I straightened and snapped around. The copywriter guy stood at the door. His jacket was gone, and his black shirt sleeves were folded and pushed up to his elbows, as if he were about to get down to work, or maybe he was showing off his forearms. One never could tell. His smile was definitely that of a predator. "Nice bathroom, isn't it?"

"Ah, yeah, really nice. Which is what you'd expect from a place like this, I suppose." I swallowed and tried to assess what he wanted. Maybe this whole situation wasn't bad— maybe I was reading too much into it because I was paranoid? "How's the copywriting going?" I laughed half-heartedly. Okay, so I wasn't quite on board with my attempt to lighten the mood and go with small talk. This would have been awkward whether or not I was helping investigate theft and murder.

The copywriter guy—I couldn't for the life of me remember his name; I really needed to pay better attention —shook his head. "Lily, Lily, Lily. You must think we're stupid. Your little disguise might have fooled Samuel momentarily, but once he knew it was you, he let us know. Loyal fellow, he is. I don't know why you bothered. Besides, I was always attending today's little marketing get together, and I would've recognised you with or without your clumsy disguise." Okay, so I hadn't been overreacting by feeling creeped out. It had been wishful thinking, but, hey, I was an optimist by nature.

If he was good at witching, he would know I had my return-to-sender spell up, which would make him cautious. There was every chance I'd get out of here unscathed if I could figure out how to get past him. I had a quick look with my witchy sight. He had a return-to-sender spell activated too. The only way I could best him in a magical fight was if I had more power than him and my return-to-sender spell was stronger than his, but after only recently recovering, I didn't want to risk it. How much did he know about my recent problems? There was a good chance he was way stronger than me because of it. Crap.

He came into the bathroom and took a couple of steps towards me. I wanted to stand my ground, show I wasn't scared, but my subconscious had other ideas. My feet moved slowly to the side. Apparently, I was going to try and edge around to the other side of the bath. So much for being brave.

He laughed. "There's nowhere to go, silly."

I looked over his shoulder at the only way out, which was kind of a ploy because when I did that, he flicked his head around. I went for my phone and grabbed it out of my back pocket. Putting in the damn passcode wasted precious time. Copywriting Guy turned back to me and shook his head. Stuff worrying about looking nonchalant —we were way past that. I shuffled quickly to the other side of the bath, putting it between us. "Hey, Siri, call Imani."

"No, you don't." Copywriting guy leapt forward and grabbed my wrist—the one with the phone in it. I went to twist out, but his grip was too firm, and he yanked me towards him.

"Shit!" My knee hit the side of the bath, and I fell. If I hadn't twisted, I would've smashed my face on the side of the bath, but I managed to hit the side with my shoulder, then splash in the whole way. The frigid water shocked the breath from me. My chest seized, and my mouth opened, filling with water. It took me a couple of seconds to get the brain-limb communications open, but once I did, I scrambled to turn around and get out.

My face broke the surface. I grabbed the sides of the bath and took a deep breath. Copywriting Guy stood there, the little fan heater buzzing away in his hand. He grinned and held it over the bath. "This is where we say goodb—"

I pushed off with my feet and sprang out of the bath, to the same side I'd been on before being dragged in. I grabbed his arm—the one not holding the heater—and I jerked with all my strength.

I jumped backwards as he landed in the bath with a splosh, spark, and sizzle. His limbs stiffened, and he twitched violently. His jaw clenched. I stood rooted to the spot, blinking. His staring eyes seemed to be fixated on me, but that was impossible.

He was dead.

My wits returned. I carefully hurried around the tub, trying not to slip on the water, and turned the heater off at the wall. Nobody else needed to get electrocuted by accident.

My teeth chattered. Oh, that's right; I was drenched and bloody freezing. Waterlogged clothes stuck to my skin and weighed me down. I peeled my coat off, with difficulty, and let it fall to the floor with a muffled splat. I could do with a heater about now. My gaze travelled to the bath and the heater floating within it. Hmm, maybe not that one. One of the lilies in the tub had floated into the grill at the front of the heater, its petals sticking out. I was pretty sure that wasn't the effect the agent had been going for. If I photographed the scene now, people would think it was a set-up. Unfortunately, they'd be wrong.

My phone was in that bath somewhere. Damn. I was not going to stick my hand in. No freaking way. And I wasn't going to use my magic to get it out because that would put my magic signature all over the scene and make it look like I'd killed him in cold... water? Well, there was no blood.

"Lily, Adrian!" came from another room. Ah, so that's what his name was. How much of the ploy to steal money was Samuel privy to? Did he even know the people he was dealing with were witches? Maybe he thought he was helping a crime syndicate but didn't know the details?

I was about to call back, then make a run for the outside

and my car, when I noticed something I couldn't believe I'd missed before. The underside of Copywriter Guy's forearm was visible just under the water. I leaned closer. A shiver wracked my body, and this time, it wasn't from the cold. Black and stark against his white skin, the letters stood out, even through their watery grave.

Regula Pythonissam.

CHAPTER 13

I ran into Samuel on my way downstairs. His eyes widened when he saw me. I narrowed mine—had he called out to subtly see who had made it out of the bathroom alive? "Surprised? Disappointed?" I asked.

"Um, I don't know what you mean. Why are you wet, and where's Adrian?"

"He's spending time in the tub. He tried to get me to go in first, but it didn't work out how he envisaged. The turn of events gave him quite a shock." I didn't have it in me to smirk. The whole thing was horrible. Once again, I'd almost been killed—which was always enough to ruin my day—and once again, I'd had to kill someone. My body count was piling up, and I wasn't even trying. Imagine if I had an agenda. Hmm, actually I did: destroy Regula Pythonissam while finding out what happened to my parents. I guessed I was working towards that, albeit slowly.

Samuel's mouth dropped open. He flinched away from me, then pushed me into the bannister so he could run past. The timber dug into my lower back, but I didn't care. I needed to get outside and find Imani. I wanted to make a doorway straight to the PIB and gather reinforcements because we couldn't let Samuel go, but I didn't have any coordinates to get back here. Maybe I could take Samuel's phone to ring Imani.

Magic prickled my scalp.

"What? No!" rang out from the bathroom. A gunshot, then silence.

My breaths came quickly. Looked as if we just lost someone to interrogate. Crap.

I had my return-to-sender spell up, but it wouldn't protect me against a gun. Nevertheless, I couldn't leave. We at least needed the evidence of Adrian's body, and the bullet that killed Samuel. I forced my feet to turn around and sneak back up the stairs.

I stopped at the top and listened. Nothing. I slowly, quietly placed my sopping coat and camera equipment on the ground. If I had to run, I could either grab them or magic them to my car. I hated to leave it all sitting alone without me, but there was nothing for it. I couldn't afford any distractions or extra weight, and I couldn't magic to my car now because whoever was upstairs would know I was still in the house, although they probably already knew because of those stupid cameras. Gah.

My heart hammered, sending my pulse thudding against my eardrums. I tried to breathe quietly, but it was damn hard. I flexed my empty hands. A weapon would be handy right about now. There was one more door on my right before the bathroom. I hadn't been in there yet and didn't know what was inside, but if it was like every other room in this mansion, it would have a fireplace and all the hard, sharp, dangerous paraphernalia that went with it.

I turned the handle and shoved the door open quickly to avoid any potential squeaks. I smiled. A bedroom. I jogged to the fireplace and snatched a poker.

Hefting it in both hands, I ran back to the door and ducked my head out to make sure the hallway was clear. It was. Here went nothing. My numbing feet squelched and slid around in my boots as I approached the bathroom door. That was such a gross feeling. *Focus, idiot.*

Taking a last deep breath, I paused outside the door, back against the wall, poker gripped in front of me. *One. Two. Go!* I jumped in front of the door and screamed— surprise was a legitimate ploy. Then I shut my mouth, weapon still ready to do some damage. But there was no one to damage. The room was empty. There wasn't anything unusual, well, except for the pool of blood on the floor.

Crap.

I RAN DOWNSTAIRS AND OUTSIDE, LEAVING MY PHONE IN THE bath, as I didn't want to mess up the crime scene. I'd grabbed my stuff from the floor, though. Now outside, the chill bit into my wet clothes. I put my equipment in my boot and whispered, "The clothes I'm wearing are sopping wet. I need them dry right now, please, and heated to Celcius thirty degrees." *Ahhhhh.* Toasty warm and dry. Now, this was witching. I wriggled my toes, which stung as they thawed out.

There was no sign of Imani anywhere in the front field, I guessed you'd call it. There was no "yard" about this place. My stomach somersaulted. Where was she? Her call had dropped out, and phone reception wasn't always fantastic, but she should've been close by, and my phone had had good reception before it died. I swallowed the urge to cry. I was not going to lose it now.

I threw my glasses into the front seat and locked the car because I might as well leave it here. It would be quicker to make a doorway to the PIB, then drive back. If I had to drive there as well, it would take twice as long. My maths ability was dodgy, but even I could work that one out.

I made my doorway, pasting the PIB coordinates in gold on my conjured door, and stepped into the PIB reception room. I pressed the intercom. The door opened, but instead of Gus, there was a tall, slim woman in her twenties. She held out the iPad-looking thing. "Hand here, please." I placed my hand on it. It beeped once, and my name and photo came up on the screen. "Who are you here to see, Miss Bianchi?" Wow, she was formal. What happened to introductions and a hello? I bet if you went to her place for dinner, she'd be straight into the main course with no cheese and dip beforehand.

"Agent Bianchi or Agent DuPree—Ma'am. This is kind of urgent."

She tilted her head. "Are you saying I should hurry?"

"Um, that's usually what urgent means." Was she stupid or just having an insecure moment where she had to show me who had the authority?

"That smart mouth won't get you anywhere. I have a mind to put you in a holding room for a while so you can think about it."

"My phone was destroyed on an assignment, and I've just killed someone in self-defence."

She snorted. "Sure you have." She rolled her eyes. "Says here"—she held up the tablet—"you're not even an agent. Have you been impersonating an agent? That's a crime, you know."

Oh for God's sake. "Are you going to call James or Ma'am for me? You know James will be pissed if you don't. He's my brother."

"Sure he is. Just because you have the same last name doesn't mean squat."

I shook my head. Imani could be dead or dying. These seconds could be the most precious ever. To get her off guard, I flicked my head around to look back down the hallway. "Oh my God, look at that!" I turned quickly back towards her. Just as I'd hoped, she was looking past me to see what had gotten my attention. That was my chance.

I bolted.

As the smack of my boots echoed through the corridor, she shouted after me, "Come back, or I'll shoot!"

What the hell? Well, I wasn't stopping now. If she killed me, she'd be in a world of trouble, and there was a corner coming up. There. I sprinted around the right-hand turn and opened the first door on the left. A middle-aged woman with large owlish glasses sat at a desk. She looked at me and pursed her lips. "Can I help you?"

"Yes, please. I'm Agent Bianchi's sister, and some crazy guard is trying to shoot me. Please can you call my brother, James, and tell him I'm here?"

She didn't even baulk, as if this kind of interruption happened all the time. "Of course I can. Just a moment."

I turned to look back at the door. I'd shut it after me, but I expected that crazy, power-mad terrier to come through at any moment.

"Hello. This is Amanda, Clementine's secretary…. Yes, is James there? No? Oh, his sister is in our office. She's having trouble getting Erin to take her to him…. Yes, of course…. Will do. Bye." She hung the phone up and looked at me, a smile spreading across her face. "Your brother's not there, but Olivia is sending Ma'am right down. Just take a seat."

"Thanks so much. I appreciate it." I sat while she went back to work typing. My leg jiggled as I stared at the door. If that guard found me first, she was liable to kill me. This was more dangerous than being on the job. The door opened, and my whole body tensed, ready to jump up and bolt. I'd spell her gun to break or something if she pointed it at me. Thankfully, Ma'am walked in. I sighed my relief and stood.

I wanted to give her a huge hug, but I refrained—it wasn't professional.

"What in heavens happened, Lily?" Ma'am stood just inside the open door.

I was about to answer when Psycho Guard's voice came from the hallway. "Ma'am. There's a fugitive in the building. I've put out a red alert. She's disobedient and dangerous. She may be armed."

You had got to be kidding me. What a lying piece of—

"Are you talking about *this* fugitive, by any chance?" Ma'am gestured in my direction. Her poker face had transformed into something that reminded me of razor blades and eggshells. Don't ask me exactly what that looks like, but you wouldn't want to make a wrong step when she was displaying that face. I was pretty sure someone was about to, though, and it took everything I had to suppress the gloating smile that desperately wanted to burst forth.

Psycho Guard edged into the room and stood next to Ma'am. Her jaw muscles bunched when she saw me, and she narrowed her eyes. The hand hanging at her side still had her gun in it.

"Still planning on shooting me?" I folded my arms and raised my brows.

Ma'am's mouth opened slightly, which was akin to a normal person dropping their jaw on the floor. Her voice rose. "You were going to what?!"

"Well, she ran. I told her to stop, and she wouldn't, so I said I'd shoot." The woman stood taller, as if that would lend her position credibility. Taking in Ma'ams thunder-cloud expression, I figured it wasn't working.

"Do you know who this young lady is?" Ma'am asked.

"She said she was Agent Bianchi's sister. But so what?"

As fun as it was to watch Ma'am tear strips off her, Imani couldn't wait. "Um, Ma'am, I'm sorry to interrupt, but Imani's missing. I was almost murdered at that house, and I killed someone in self-defence. We need to get back there now."

The secretary behind the desk drew in a sharp breath, and Ma'am turned back to me, poker face in place. "Do we have coordinates?"

"No." I told her the address.

She shook her head. "I'm afraid we'll have to do this the non-witch way. Follow me." Just before we left, she scowled at the stupid guard. "You're on leave, effective immediately. There will be an enquiry into your conduct. Leave your gun at reception." As we marched past her, I finally gave in to my gloating smile. And boy did it feel good.

As we hurried to the lift and car park, Ma'am got on her phone and gathered the troops. At least this was in more capable hands than mine now, but unease cramped my stomach.

Was it too late for Imani?

CHAPTER 14

Ma'am put a no-notice spell on our Porsche—
even she seemed to be partial to the charm of
the pretty sportscar—so we could speed to our
destination without attracting police attention. As she
changed lanes onto the wrong side of the road to overtake a
red Mini, I gripped the door and gritted my teeth. "Um,
won't other people not see us and drive into our path?"

"I made it so only police don't notice us, and we're invisible to radar. The average person will see us. Don't worry,
dear."

Easy for her to say—she was the crazy-fast driver. As she
took a sweeping bend, my side plastered against my door.
My life had never felt more out of my control—both figura-
tively and literally. But I didn't say anything else. Imani's life
was at stake, if she was even still alive, and if we were late by

a few seconds, I didn't want to be the reason. Ma'am was a good driver, but I was betting she needed to concentrate while in racing mode.

We finally arrived at the estate. The car kicked up a lot of dust as Ma'am gunned it down the long gravel driveway. She threw the handbrake on and slid one-eighty degrees to a stop. I slapped my hand on my chest. "For the love of God. Since when did you turn into a hoon?"

She raised a brow. "Whatever do you mean, dear?" Her voice was as composed and calm as if I'd just questioned her choice of tea. "My driving skills are impeccable."

I rolled my eyes. I supposed my heart rate would return to normal eventually. "Whatever. So how do we find Imani?"

Another car, a black BMW SUV, sped down the driveway and stopped a couple of car lengths away. Three black-uniformed agents jumped out. Ma'am gave a nod and opened her door. "These lads will help us. Just a moment, dear. When I'm finished, you can show me through the house. We'll go over things as they happened." Without waiting for my answer, she hopped out and met the men at the bonnet of our car.

I got out and eavesdropped. There was probably nothing I could add to help, but you never knew. By the sounds of things, though, they had a decent plan. They'd tracked her phone to this property, but whether we'd find her with her phone was another thing. Wings of panic fluttered in my chest. *Please be okay.* I hurried to my car and got my camera out of the boot. I'd never tried to get photos of things that had just happened, but I didn't see why it wouldn't work. The past was the past. I returned the Porsche.

"Okay. Stay connected," Ma'am said.

One of the agents nodded. "Yes, Ma'am." He mumbled something, and he and another of them ran off, towards the left side of the house.

Ma'am and the third agent stayed with me. "Time to show me what happened, Lily."

Ma'am was young for her age—not that I knew exactly how old she was—so I jogged, knowing she'd easily be able to keep up. The front door was still unlocked. In the vestibule, I called out, "Hello! Anyone home?" What if the owners had no idea of what had gone on? That was assuming they were still alive. This whole scheme had gone pear-shaped pretty quickly. The owners could be oblivious and out shopping, or dead. What a mess.

No one answered. I turned to Ma'am. "All the bad stuff happened in the upstairs bathroom." I hurried up the stairs. The poker was still where I left it on the floor in the hallway. The pool of blood had begun to seep into the timber floor. I approached the bath, careful to avoid treading in any of the blood. My phone sat at the bottom of the tub, face down. I didn't want to grab it and sully any evidence.

"So this is it?"

"Yes. The copywriter guy's name was Adrian. He shoved me into the bath and tried to throw a heater in with me, but I jumped out just in time, then grabbed him and pulled him in. He was holding the heater, which was on, and he fried."

I told her what happened with the agent, Samuel, and how another witch had arrived, that I'd heard a gunshot, but all the bodies were missing when I'd returned with the poker.

I wanted to take photos, but that other agent was standing there, and we didn't want details of my talent getting out. The less everyone knew about my special power, the better. I wasn't even sure about mentioning the Regula Pythonissam tattoo. How much had Ma'am told the other agents? And who did she trust? We were generally operating with the assumption that we couldn't trust anyone except those sworn in at James's place, which was Imani, Olivia, Will, Beren, Millicent, Ma'am, and James. That was a tiny proportion of PIB agents.

Ma'am turned to the agent, who had stayed watching from the hallway. "Agent Barber, could you secure the house, please? I'm going to call in the forensics team. And find out who owns this place. We need to contact them."

"Yes, Ma'am." He slid his phone out of his inside jacket pocket and strode down the hallway, towards the stairs.

Once he was gone, I stood at the doorway. "Show me Adrian, after I killed him." His body appeared in the bath, the heater with him. I clicked off a shot and shuddered. Without looking away—I didn't want to risk losing the image—I walked in an arc to my left, well away from where I knew the blood was. When I reached the other side of the bath, I leaned closer and took a picture of the tattoo and another one of his face. The dead, staring eyes made me gag. I lowered the camera and took a few deep breaths.

"Are you all right?"

I nodded and swallowed. "I'll be fine." I went to the hallway, just outside the door, and raised the camera again —I needed to finish before the forensics guys arrived. "Show me in the bath." Adrian's back was to me. He stood over the bath as I looked up at him, my hands on the sides of the tub. It was weird seeing myself in one of these pictures. And even though I knew I'd been terrified, it only just showed through my angry face. I actually looked like I was about to unleash hell. And I had. I smiled, proud of myself. *Click. Click.*

Not wanting to waste time, I then said, "Show me who killed Samuel." Samuel's back was to me, and he raised his hands. Crap! I flicked my camera to video mode and pressed the shutter button to start recording.

The warmth of my magic trickled from my stomach, up through my chest, to my scalp. This was definitely drawing more power than taking photos, but if I channelled it to the river of magic, maybe I could conserve more of my own energy. I opened the portal to the river wider and drew from it.

Adrian was still in the bath, and the newcomer stood behind it, facing Samuel. My mouth dropped open, and I sucked in a loud breath.

"Lily, what is it?"

The guy behind the bath was the same guy who'd been in the photos with Piranha at the warehouse during the tea incident. This was all related somehow. Were they the witch equivalent to the Mafia? "I'm videoing. Hang on."

I carefully edged to the left of Samuel. Filming from the

side would get both of their facial expressions, although I had to stick close to the wall to get them both in, and even then, I had to pan from one to the other. Right now, the new guy pointing the gun at Samuel was talking. I didn't think the voices would come up in filming later, but you never knew. My magic was full of surprises. And assuming it didn't have any good surprises, we might be able to read his lips later. His lips stopped moving and curled into an evil smile.

I moved the camera to get Samuel's face. He said something. His eyes widened. Putting his hands up in a placating move, he shook his head, and now it was clear he was saying, no, no, no. The gun moved into shot. A flash, and Samuel stumbled backwards, clutching his stomach. He fell to his knees and dropped onto his side. Everything froze. That must be it. I filmed for a few more seconds, just in case it was like the Marvel movies where there were outtakes or extra stuff after the credits, but no, nothing more to see here.

I pressed the shutter button and stopped filming. As usual, I had impeccable timing because I could hear voices coming up the stairs. "Are you done?" Ma'am asked.

"Yes. Let's go downstairs, and I'll show you the footage."

We passed the two forensics guys on the way down, and Ma'am stopped to have a quick chat. I kept going—there was no reason for me to eavesdrop this time. Ma'am joined me a minute later, and we wandered into the games room. I created a bubble of silence. "Here are the photos. The last one is a video. I've turned the sound up, just in case. I couldn't hear anything when I was filming, but you never know. My magic is mysterious, especially to me." I smiled.

Ma'am looked at the photos, then pressed Play on the video. Oh. My. God! The voices came through. Ma'am nodded. One corner of her mouth turned up. My grin, however, was huge. I guessed it was too much to ask for her to have more than an understated reaction, but I wasn't going to let it ruin my excitement. This was huge. At least *I* thought it was.

The Greek-looking guy with the neck tattoo said, "We can no longer do business. And your friend here has managed to stuff everything up."

Samuel's forehead wrinkled. "He was never my friend. And I've done everything you asked."

"It wasn't enough."

And there Samuel was, putting up his hands, trying to plead his case. "But we got you those properties. No, no, no!"

Bang!

He fell to the floor, and the picture on the screen froze.

Ma'am's voice was quiet as she said, "What's their overall agenda?"

Was she talking to herself, or did she expect me to answer? "I don't know, but they seem to be doing things that affect non-witches."

She turned her sharp gaze on me. "Ah, but not always. Your mother is missing, and they've tried to kidnap you. Today—I'm sure it hasn't escaped your notice—they tried to kill you."

"Maybe it's just because I got in their way, or maybe they weren't supposed to kill me?"

"Wishful thinking, dear. As it stands, we have to assume the worst. And what have they done with Imani?"

I looked out of the glass doors to the grounds beyond. Was she out there, or had they taken her somewhere? She had to be alive. And where was Will? While I was at it, I might as well ask why we had to die at all. Sheesh, life was a depressing farce sometimes.

Ma'am's phone rang. "Yes?" She listened for a minute, then turned to me. "Which way to the back garden?"

"Through here." I hurried to the next room and to the doors facing the back of the property. I tried them, but they were locked. Asking for a rhyme on such short notice was impossible. "Please unlock the doors." A zap of power shot out through my hand, shocking me. I snatched my hand back, and the door opened by itself.

Ma'am smiled. "Nice one, dear. Now please get out of my way." I stepped to the side, then followed her through. She jogged for a couple of hundred metres, to where a large brick shed stood surrounded by short topiary balls. The shed was about the size of a triple garage. We entered from the side door.

Imani! The two agents from earlier were standing on either side of her. She sat with her back against a tractor wheel—the wheel was still attached to the tractor. I ran to her and dropped to my knees. "Are you all right? What happened?" I placed my hands on her shoulders and looked her over, checking for wounds or blood. There were none, thank God.

She looked at me, her eyes red and unfocussed. She squinted, shook her head, and winced. "I have the worst blinking headache." She placed her head in her hands and groaned.

"What can you tell me?" Ma'am asked the two agents who found her.

The taller one answered, "She was lying on the ground, stiff as a board. Her arms and legs were straight—she'd been tied with magic, couldn't move. We asked her what happened, but she doesn't remember."

Ma'am knelt next to me and put her hands on either side of Imani's head. Ma'am stared into the distance, then shut her eyes. Familiar warmth vibrated my scalp. While she did that, one of the agents dialled someone on his phone. "Agent Minter here. Can you get agent Beren DuPree into the clinic? Yes, under Ma'am's request. It's urgent. Thank you." He hung up as Ma'am opened her eyes.

She angry-snorted out her nose and pressed her lips together. "I'm afraid her memories of the last few days have been wiped. Such an imprecise spell. Damn fools who use it. We're lucky more isn't missing. There aren't too many witches who can do that spell without wiping half the person's memories out. Whoever did this was competent, but not great. They managed to only wipe a few days, but I'm betting it's a few more days than they were trying to get rid of. At least there's no other damage. She's going to have a migraine until we can get Beren to heal her." She stood. "Boys, please get her back to the PIB and my nephew."

Imani gave me a weak wave before one of the agents bent down and gently grabbed her arm. He must have made his doorway around them because they disappeared. The other agent stepped through his doorway, and Ma'am turned to me. "Time to get to work. Are you ready to take some photos?"

Was I ever.

I shouldn't have been so keen though. "Show me who tied Imani up." Two men appeared—the guy with the neck tattoo who killed Samuel stood facing the camera, but another man in black stood with his back to me. I swallowed. I knew I'd been missing Will, but now strangers were reminding me of him. This guy was a similar height. His broad shoulders, and the way he stood, his proportions, all reminded me of the man I missed like crazy.

I carefully walked around until I could see the man's face. *Click. Click.* "God, no."

"Lily? What is it?" It was as if Ma'am's voice came from Jupiter through a voice-mashing fog. Was I still in the real world? Maybe I was, but my heart wasn't. It had gone to Hell and left me here with a chunk missing, and my breakfast wanted freedom. I swallowed against its attempt.

I took one more photo and lowered the camera. Not bothering to hide the tears spilling over my lashes, I handed her the camera. "See for yourself." Even my voice came out dead.

She looked at the screen, and her mouth fell open.

When she looked at me, I expected her to say something, make some excuse, or tell me it couldn't possibly be Will standing over Imani, helping our enemy. But she said nothing. Which was the last thing I wanted to hear.

My throat had closed, and my next question barely escaped. "Now what?"

She set her jaw, and her nostrils flared. "We go and save some homeowners."

CHAPTER 15

We both kept our own counsel on the drive to the first house. How could Will betray us like that? Surely he had a good reason. But why wouldn't he just come home and tell us what was happening if he knew? And did he know they'd tried to kill me and had still done nothing? I shook my head. Not my Will. *No, not your Will. Maybe he'd never been your Will?* I bit my tongue, trying to stop my tears—I didn't want red eyes at the next appointment.

After what seemed like a bazillion miles, we pulled up in front of a neat home. Ma'am got out first and led the way to the house. I followed, camera in hand. We were going to pretend to be from the agency since no one would know Samuel had disappeared yet, so the owners would have been expecting us. Our aim was to remove all the haunting devices and stop any more unwanted property sales. Something good had to come out of today, or what was the point?

The man who answered the door to the semi-detached cottage asked why we were forty minutes late. "I'm so sorry," said Ma'am, smiling. "Our last client kept us back, and we strive to make sure everything is perfect for our clients. We'll reduce your fee by two hundred quid. Here." She fished in her pocket and pulled out the money. What the hell? She handed it over.

The man's eyes widened. He smiled and took the money. "Come in. Come in, please. I'm just glad your clients matter to you so much."

Ma'am went in first and turned to me. "You know what to do, dear." She smiled and then turned to the man, taking his arm in a friendly way to lead him to wherever the sitting room was—poker-face champion and now acclaimed actress. I didn't know where she pulled that smile from. I'm sure mine had left for a holiday until next year. Her wonderful ability—not just with finding smiles when she needed them—was going to get us information. If his house had been haunted, she was going to spell him into forgetting that had ever been an issue and make him decide not to sell.

I visited each room, panning my camera around and taking photos of the invisible cameras. Once satisfied I'd found all of them, I repeated a spell Ma'am showed me just before we'd gotten in the car. "Spying devices be gone, make this house an unhaunted home." Once the tingle of the spell had faded, I lifted my camera and pointed it at where I'd seen one of the cameras. "Show me the hidden camera." It was gone. I repeated this for all the spots. I'd done it! One house down, three to go... at least three we knew of and had appointments to. Ma'am had one of the other PIB agents sifting through Samuel's office to find out all the other places they'd been in the middle of targeting.

After saying goodbye to the homeowner, who'd decided not to sell but was also two hundred quid richer, we went to the next house. Ma'am received a call on the way. Once she got off the phone, she turned to me and smiled. "We beat them to Samuel's files. We've got twenty-eight properties to go."

Why was she smiling? I was going to be dead once it was over. Twenty-eight! "I hope you're going to help with the spells. I'm tired already, what with everything that happened this morning."

"Don't worry, dear. I'll do my share. Why don't you call my nephew and see how Imani is doing?" Her kindnesses surprised me because I was used to her cracking the whip, but I should've known she really cared about all of us—she'd demonstrated that time and again over the last few months. And surely she was hurting almost as much as I was at Will's betrayal, but she'd pushed it to the side to do her job.

I dialled Beren. He picked up quickly, thank God. "Hey, how's the patient?"

He took an audible breath. "She's good, other than her missing memories. I did find a magic signature though, one that's in our database."

"Oh my God, that's wonderful! When do we arrest the

evil witch?" Unless that evil witch was Will. I shut my eyes. This was getting worse.

He lowered his voice. "It's not quite that simple. There's something else too. I need more time with Imani to sift through, go further into the network of memories. Just tell Ma'am we'll need to have a meeting when she's done in the field."

I didn't want to ask anything specific in case he wasn't talking about Will. I didn't think blurting out about his betrayal over the phone was any way to tell his best friend what was going on. I'd have to hold it in until tonight. "Oh. Why do you sound so worried?"

"I can't talk about it now. I'll see you later. Okay?"

"Ah, okay." I scrunched my forehead. I hoped Beren's news wasn't going to make me hate Will even more. Although I wasn't sure I hated him. I was angry, yes, but I couldn't make up my mind how I felt because maybe this was all part of his undercover gig? I sighed.

"Be careful out there, Lil. Promise?"

"Yes, of course."

"Bye." He hung up.

I looked over at Ma'am, who was focussed on the road. A mist of dread filtered through my lungs until it was hard to breathe. Something was very, very wrong.

Without taking her eyes from the road, Ma'am asked, "What's wrong, dear?"

"I don't know. Beren hasn't finished with Imani. She's okay, for the most part, but Beren thinks he knows who hurt her. He says we have their magical signature on file."

Her shoulders slumped.

"Are you thinking what I'm thinking?"

She sighed heavily. "Probably. If the who is who I think it is, the why will be most important, which is probably Beren's problem. He needs to find out the why before we discuss the who." Strangely, that made total sense. "Now's not the time to talk about it, dear. We have some work to do yet."

"Bu—"

"No buts, I'm afraid. Just trust me on this. If it's any consolation, we should have an answer tonight. Beren's rather resourceful when he sets his mind to it."

It wasn't really any consolation because when I studied Ma'am's side profile, there was nothing poker-faced about it. She looked like a woman who had all her money on the table and a hand of cards she wished she hadn't been dealt.

I stared out the window as we passed fields and houses, random strangers going about their happy lives. Why couldn't I be one of those oblivious people? Maybe someone riding a horse or having a picnic, even someone milking a cow and worrying about getting their product to market. Instead, I had the most horrible feeling that when the cards fell, we were going to lose... big time.

By 7:00 p.m. we'd covered half the houses. As Ma'am drove us back to the PIB, my eyes shut, and I yawned. My magic had exhausted me physically, and this whole thing

with Will had exhausted me emotionally. My condition could be described as totally wrecked. Would I ever recover? If Will had defected to the other side, what did that mean? Would we be after him now? How could we all ignore we cared about him and try and capture him, maybe kill him trying? And if he had done this to pretend to be in with the group, how low would he have to stoop to find what we needed and not get killed? Pain throbbed in my forehead.

At least the problem of Mrs Soames had been solved. Her house would be our last job when we returned home tonight. We would banish the witch haunting her house. We hadn't worked out exactly what spells they'd used to do it without leaving a magical trace, but we'd get there. Maybe there was something built into the camera equipment? Instead of disappearing all of them from Mrs Soames, we should grab a couple and study them in the lab.

Ma'am parked in the underground car park, and as we went up in the lift, my stomach gurgled.

"Someone's hungry. When was the last time you ate?"

"Breakfast." That was about eleven hours ago, but seeing as Will had destroyed my desire to do anything that would prolong my life, eating was counterproductive.

"We'll have dinner while we have the meeting."

The doors opened, and we got out. "That's okay. I'm not hungry."

She grabbed my arm and stopped us in the hallway. She turned me to face her. "Lily, you can't go without eating. We need you strong. We have all those houses to clear tomorrow, and Mrs Soames's tonight. I know you're concerned about

WITCH HAUNTED IN WESTERHAM

Will, but you can't let it affect you to the point it's self-destructive."

I searched for my anger at being told what to do, but I found nothing. "I'm sorry. I'm just not hungry. I'll still do everything you need me to."

"You need to toughen up. Your happiness is not dictated by your relationship with Will, or any man, for that matter. Why do you fight in the first place?"

I shrugged. "Because I want to help people. And when unfair things happen to people, it really ticks me off."

"Right. So don't let whatever this is stop that from happening. We need you healthy, Lily. I may be selfish demanding this of you, but we need you. So much more is at stake than even I realise. But it will come to light soon. I'm sure of it. Don't forget your parents. Your mother wouldn't approve of you giving up."

Bam. Bullseye. It was a dirty move but effective. "Okay, I'll eat something. Maybe if it's a double-chocolate muffin and coffee, or I could go for some Indian."

She smiled. "That's better, dear. Now come on. Everyone's waiting for us." She mumbled something and set off down the hall. I reluctantly followed because not *everyone* was waiting for us. Will wouldn't be there. Gah, now I sounded pathetic even to myself. I just didn't want to believe he'd abandoned us for Piranha. He had ethics. In fact, he was one of the most reliable, fair people I'd ever met. I had to believe there was a good reason he'd done whatever he'd done. And the connection between us… I hadn't imagined it. He wouldn't walk away from that willingly.

I took a deep breath and tipped my chin up, literally. I was going to assume the best until the worst was proven. My mother would expect nothing less.

When we walked into the conference room, Olivia took one look at me and ran over. "Are you okay? You look terrible."

I laughed. "You always know how to make me feel special."

She blushed. "Oh, gosh, I didn't mean that. Sorry! I just mean—"

"It's okay. I know what you meant. And I'll explain later. I want to hear what Beren has to say first." I met his gaze over her shoulder. He gave a gentle nod, but his sad eyes reflected my own state of mind. Olivia hooked her arm through mine and led me to the table. She sat next to Beren, and I sat on her other side.

My brother's smile was small, but at least it was there. "Hey. I heard you've had an eventful day. Are you okay?"

"Yeah, kind of. I'm tired." My stomach gurgled again. "And hungry."

"So predictable." He winked. I rolled my eyes, but I appreciated him trying to cheer me up. A bit of light-hearted banter was welcome.

Millicent sat next to him. I guess this conversation was big enough for us all to hear. "Look at your tummy! It's only been a week since I saw you last."

She patted the offending lump and grinned. "It won't stop moving either, especially at night. I'll be happy when it's out; then I won't be the only one not getting enough sleep." She tipped her head towards James.

The only one who wasn't here was Imani. I looked across Olivia to Beren. "How's Imani? Will she be all right?"

"Yes. She'll be fine, but she's asleep. I actually managed to recover some of her memories. Delving so deep isn't only taxing for me. She probably won't wake up until tomorrow. We have her safe."

"That's good. So they didn't do anything else?" If Will had hit her or worse, I didn't think I could ever forgive him.

"You mean physically? No. They tied her up, then put her to sleep, and wiped her memory, all with magic. There were no wounds or blunt-force trauma."

I blew out a huge breath. Olivia squeezed my hand. Did she know what part Will had played?

"Right," Angelica said. "Let's eat." Food appeared on the table. From the scents wafting over me, there was Indian, chocolate, coffee, and cinnamon. A plate had come out of nowhere and sat in front of me, waiting to be filled. There was also a takeout coffee cup next to my right hand with a Costa emblem on it.

I looked at Ma'am. "How did you do this? I thought it was stealing if you just popped food from somewhere."

She smiled. "Don't be ridiculous. There's a witch service that has an account with witchy food providers, and they take what they want; then their account is charged. We pay the account of the person who arranges for this to appear. They're called Witcheroo."

"Oh, like Deliveroo but, yeah."

She smiled. "They're owned by the same company. Anyway, dig in. We'll have a chat when we've finished eating." She raised her brows, giving that statement emphasis. I was pretty sure that was an order to eat rather than a suggestion.

I grabbed some rice and spooned beef vindaloo over the top. I also magicked a glass of water to myself because you never knew how hot vindaloo was going to be—and yes, I knew people said milk was better for extinguishing a curry inferno, but ew, not with dinner. I sniffed the delicious fragrance before forking some into my mouth. It set a small fire, but it wasn't anything I couldn't handle. Once I started eating, I realised how famished I was—sad or not, I really did need food. When I'd finished dinner, I grabbed dessert —a double-chocolate muffin and the coffee. Once everyone was finished, Ma'am waved her arm and magicked the rubbish away.

"Right, time to get down to business." She fixed her gaze on Beren. "I understand you have some important news regarding what you found in Imani's mind. As a precursor, I'd like to enlighten you all as to what happened today. In fact, I'll get Lily to start." She nodded at me.

I started my story at the beginning of this morning, which now seemed like a week ago. So much had happened, none of it good. That wasn't exactly a fair balance, but the universe wasn't known as being a fair master. When I got to the part about almost being electrocuted in the bath, James's face drained of colour. I shrugged. "You know anything can happen out in the field. I told you that I didn't want to be an agent, but you guys keep asking me to do things. Besides, people need help, and what good is my talent if I refuse?"

He shook his head. "It doesn't make it any easier. If you died…." Millicent reached out and took his hand in hers. At least he had his family if anything happened to me.

"Anyway, after I killed him, I met Samuel on the stairs." Hmm, that sounded blasé, like killing people meant as much to me as making coffee, which was far from the truth. The mantle of sadness draped over me seemed to get heavier whenever I thought about it. Guilt was a good thing—it meant I was still me. If I ever did get to the point where I didn't care, I wasn't worth anything to anyone, least of all myself.

I told them the rest of what happened upon my arrival at the PIB. Ma'am took over, explaining about finding Imani and what my photos had shown. "Please show everyone the photos, dear."

I passed my camera to Olivia, and it slowly made its way around the table, everyone's faces contorting in surprise and confusion as they recognised Will. I sighed and let my frown take over. Why bother hiding how I felt? Everyone else probably felt the same.

After James had perused the photos, he slid my camera across the table to me. Angelica folded her arms. "We won't dissect Will's motives just yet. I want to hear from Beren first. I have a feeling he's going to be able to answer some of the questions we have. As bad as this looks, we all know Will, and in my experience, he's not going to disappoint us. So, Agent DuPree, what did you find?"

I swallowed. *Please be good news.* My leg bounced up and down, and I resisted the urge to bite my fingernails. Beren cleared his throat. "The magic signature I found on Imani was Will's. He bound her and wiped her memories. He had to make the memory thing look a bit clumsier so it would look like someone else did it. That's my estimation anyway. The other thing he did was to implant a false memory of a conversation he never had with Imani."

Okay, so that actually made sense. If the guy standing over him making him do everything was watching, Will couldn't have told her what he really wanted to say. I guess that was my hopeful version. The other reason could be because Will was guilty and wanted to point the finger at someone else. But he wouldn't be so obvious about it then, would he? Gah. *Stop thinking, Lily.*

Beren continued, "I'm assuming Will wouldn't have had time to implant much, but his message to us using his exact words was, 'Trust me. But be wary.'"

I wrinkled my brow. What did that mean? Trust him but don't? "Um, were they two separate things, or does he want us to trust him but not?"

Ma'am nodded slowly. "He wants us to trust him, but something else is coming. It's hard implanting memories, especially after wiping some. He would have had a couple of seconds, if that, and when you implant memories, you can accidentally overwrite other ones. He's done the best he could. So we do what he's asked: we trust him, and we watch out for something else that's coming from the snake group. Whatever it is, I'm sure he's doing his best to stop it, but I imagine he has little to no influence. I wanted him to gather information, not blow the whole thing open wide by himself when he has no support."

"So now what?" I asked.

"Tonight we clear Mrs Soames's place of *ghosts*." She rolled her eyes, then smirked at me. "I told you they didn't exist."

"Yeah, yeah. And I believed you, except for that guy who almost killed Imani and me. And we weren't the only ones fooled. How many homes have we seen today?"

Her poker face came back. "Yes, I know. So, tomorrow you and I have to clear out some more homes, and then there will be an investigation into Samuel's murder, although I'm hoping Will can help us with that when he resurfaces. At this stage, the regular police will be notified of his disappearance by his family, I would imagine. When that comes through, I'll notify my guys there about what we know."

Worry for Will gnawed on my insides, but I pushed it away. I needed to use my energy to problem-solve right now. Stressing wasn't going to get him back to us safely. "I'd just like to mention, in case no one else noticed, that guy who was involved in Piranha's tea debacle was there today, with Will, and he killed Samuel. Should we be trying to find him?"

James looked at me. "Piranha?"

Olivia giggled. "Didn't you know? Lily calls her Dana Piranha."

"Why?" He narrowed his eyes and lifted one side of his top lip in a way that asked me if I was stupid.

"It rhymes, plus she likes eating her own kind. She's vicious, and she has sharp teeth."

He shook his head. "You're a nutter."

I shrugged. "It's only a bad thing if you want to think it is." I grinned.

He shook his head, then turned to Ma'am. "So that snake guy has managed to keep his magic signature off everything because he's gotten Will to do his dirty work for him. Did you test the magic in the bathroom?"

"The forensics guys would have, but I haven't gotten the results. I'll see if they're finished." Ma'am pulled out her phone and made a call. "Jeffrey, yes…. I am, actually." She drummed her fingers on the table while the guy talked. "Right. If you could have them on my desk by tomorrow morning. Yes. Highly classified. Tell no one. Thank you." She put her phone on the table. "We have no magic signatures in the bathroom. The only person we can implicate in this whole thing is Will, but no one knows that we have other evidence." She looked at me pointedly. "Although, as you know, we can't reveal that evidence to anyone unless we can come up with a good excuse as to how we managed to be in a position to take the photos without anyone seeing us."

"Could we maybe say I came up with a spell to take a photo of the bathroom when I couldn't be there? The barn would be a stretch, although maybe we could say there were security cameras there that the snake group missed—providing we catch the guy, and we need an excuse?"

"That's a possibility since we don't have to explain how

we managed to photograph an event that happened ten years ago. You were there when it happened. The photo from the barn is another matter though. It would be wonderful to show that Will was there with someone else— prove duress—but it would be video footage, not still shots, and we can't fabricate that. Besides, Will has immunity at the moment because he's undercover. Everything is highly classified—you're the only people who know about any of this or Will's involvement, and I'd like to keep it that way."

We all nodded. No one wanted to jeopardise Will's safety, and most of the people around the table were seasoned agents. The only non-agents were Olivia and me, and we were totally trustworthy, which Ma'am knew, or we wouldn't be sitting here.

Beren sat forward and directed his question to Ma'am. "How were they haunting the houses?"

"We haven't quite worked that out yet. I've asked the forensics guys to grab one of the cameras Lily found at the mansion today, and tonight, we'll grab the whole system from Mrs Soames's place. There might have been projectors as well as spying apparatuses. As for the traces of magic left over from them moving things, we'll have to work it out. We didn't search Mrs Soames's place after we were attacked that night, but we'll investigate tonight. If they used a strong spell, we'll find traces. Does anyone have any other questions?"

I wanted to ask when Will could come home, and whether this would all be over if we caught that guy from the snake group, but she couldn't answer those questions.

Was that guy acting alone, or was he under orders from Dana? And if so, would this ever be over? Would they start their little haunting scheme somewhere else? And why? Were they just trying to make money, or was there something even more sinister going on? My head throbbed.

"Hey, girl, stop thinking. Those wrinkles are going to be permanent if you don't relax." Olivia looked at me, concern in her eyes.

I rubbed my forehead. "I'm sorry. There's just so much we don't know. What if we can't catch that guy and this happens somewhere else?"

Ma'am interrupted. "We're not the only PIB around, dear. We have branches in other countries. I'll put the word through to watch out for similar schemes, okay?"

I nodded. That was better than nothing, but it led me to other questions. How big was this snake group, and how far was its reach? Gah, at this rate, I'd never get rid of my headache. Weariness drained each of my limbs, and the need to lie down and sleep became overwhelming.

No one else asked anything, so I stood, despite my body's protests. If I'd listened to it, I'd have crawled under the table for a nap, like we used to do as kids when we stayed out at dinner with our parents past our bedtime. "Ma'am, can we get this house clearing over and done with? I'm exhausted, and tomorrow's going to be horrible too."

"Right you are, Lily. Thanks, team. We'll gather together tomorrow night for another update meeting, and, Beren, can you have Imani attend? I'm giving her tomorrow off—Lily will be with me, so Imani can rest."

"Will do, Ma'am."

Ma'am and I said our goodbyes and went to the basement. With Mrs Soames at home, we couldn't use the reception room, and we had a lot of houses to get to tomorrow, so the car it was. At least the Porsche was nice—I wasn't a snob, but I could appreciate luxury if I had to.

The car was obviously comfortable because I fell asleep within five minutes. By the time we pulled into our driveway, and I opened my eyes, I'd managed to drool onto my jacket. I didn't want to get out into the freezing night, and I sat there as Angelica hopped out. She bent down to look back inside at me. "What are you doing?"

"I'm tired. I don't wanna get out." I affected a whiney child's voice. Maybe she'd shut the door and let me get some more sleep.

She sighed. "I'm sorry. I know you've had a hard day, but we've just got this one last thing to do." I didn't move. "Come on. I got you all the food you loved for dinner. Surely that counts for something?"

I looked at her, and guilt nipped my heart. She had dark circles under her eyes—she was almost as tired as I was, by the looks of it. Damn. "All right. You win."

She smiled, and I slid out of the car and shut the door. "Brrr, it's bloody cold."

"It is almost winter, dear. That would be why."

"Ha ha, thanks for pointing that out."

"Ready?"

I held my camera up. "Ready."

We walked across the road, and Angelica magicked the

door open, as we hadn't gotten the key from Mrs Soames. I didn't think either of us wanted the added annoyance of chatting to her first. Plus, it wasn't a good idea to get her hopes up until we knew it had worked—she was ridiculously vocal when she had something to be upset about. I did expect it to work, though, and I had gotten *my* hopes up. Fingers crossed for a sleep-in tomorrow.

There wasn't a camera in the hallway, but when I photographed her bedroom, I found one. There wasn't one in the bathroom—no one wanted to watch that—so I continued into the second bedroom—found one camera— and living room, where there were two. I was pointing out to Ma'am where they were—I didn't want to show her the photos in case the snake group was watching, and they figured out that my talent revolved around my camera.

I was about to head to the kitchen when a figure appeared—the fat, half-naked ghost. Great, just what I needed to cap off a truly craptastic day. We hadn't worked out how to get rid of it last time, but then, we'd thought we were dealing with a real ghost—at least, I had. As the beastly sight floated towards us, a sick smile beaming from his see-through face, I risked a glance at Angelica, hoping for some guidance. She gave me her poker face and turned back to watch the "ghost." So it was every witch for herself. What should I do?

I started by conjuring my return-to-sender spell, and I could see the symbol wrapped up in Angelica's aura too, so at least I'd done something right. We were in the middle of the lounge room, and there were two of us and one of him.

When Angelica stepped to the right, I stepped to the left—it made total sense to surround him if we could.

The ghost floated in front of the wall and glided to the left—well, his left, my right—so he was directly in front of me. No prizes for who he guessed was weaker. He was probably correct—Angelica had way more experience, and I was still weakened from my near-death thing and today's efforts. I didn't like my chances of beating this guy by myself. If Angelica wasn't here, I'd be running away about now.

"Hey, bozo," I said, "put a shirt on." Taunting had never worked as a defence strategy before, and I had no idea why I thought it would work now, but at least it got out some of my nervous energy.

He roared. A picture on the wall to my left dropped and smashed on the floor. More glass. The witch-ghost laughed, his hairy man boobs and stomach jiggling. His glowing yellow eyes—did I forget to mention that last time—turned to me. The glow seemed to pulse when he spoke. "You're first." Some of the glass shards, long, sharp, deadly things, floated into the air and pointed at me. Crap. My return-to-sender spell wouldn't work against those—they weren't a spell; they were real things. Even if a spell propelled them, they could still be fatal.

My scalp prickled. Out of the corner of my eye, I could see Angelica's lips moving. I didn't just want to leave it to her. I needed to protect myself—the fear icing my veins demanded I take action. I mumbled, "Disassemble the glass, and make it harmless sand." Power shot from my fingers. The glass glowed blue. The shards became the sandy colour of, well, wet sand, and then fell to the ground with little splots. There was a loud rustling behind me, and I spun. Oops. My magic hadn't been discerning. The windowpanes had turned to sand, which lay clumped on the floor.

The witch-ghost screamed. I slammed my hands over my ears and pivoted around—I should never have taken my eyes off him. He flew towards me, crashing into me, knocking me down. I slammed into the ground, back first. "Oomph." His solid mass landed on top of me, forcing the air from my lungs. Which was weird. He had substance. He'd knocked me over and was squashing me. His body had been way firmer than I'd thought a ginormous stomach would be too. And even though I was having trouble wriggling out from under him, he was not nearly as heavy as I expected such a big person to be.

I was almost free when he shifted and sat on my stomach again, legs on either side of me. He reached down and gripped my throat. Just as he tightened his fingers, cutting off my air supply, Angelica, turning, kicked him in the face. His hands released as he fell backwards. She didn't let up, though. She forced him onto his stomach on the floor and bent his arm behind his back till he screamed. Then she pulled the other arm around and said, "Cuffs on." The magic-blocking PIB cuffs appeared on his wrists. Angelica stood and put her foot on his back. He lay with his head turned to the side, blood trickling from his nose. And then something else happened....

The fat ghostly form seemed to drip away and dissolve until we were looking at the guy who'd killed Samuel. Oh my God. Had we really caught him? Okay, so Angelica had done all the work. Now we could get some answers. Was he the missing piece of the puzzle that would help us bring Dana and her group down?

Angelica read him his rights whilst dragging him off the floor. He resisted the whole way, turning this way and that, even trying to headbutt her face with the back of his skull. "Settle down," she cautioned. "Do you want me to break something else?"

"I don't care what you do to me. I won't be alive much longer. You have no idea who you're dealing with. You'll never stop us."

Angelica ignored his little speech and told her phone to call headquarters. She paused and stared into space briefly, then mumbled something. The tingle on the back of my neck lasted only a second, and then she said a string of numbers. "Okay, see them soon. Yes, four agents. Thanks."

She hung up and slid her phone into her pocket. The air shimmered in front of me, and a form appeared. I was exhausted, but I repeated my return-to-sender spell. It was probably just the agents coming to take him away, but I wasn't taking the chance.

But then I sucked in a breath, my heart frantically beating.

Will.

His gaze caught mine, a fountain of regret and grief. He shook his head but said not a word before turning, then calling down a zap of lightning to fry our prisoner. The man screamed for a second, then lay still, eyes wide. Dead. The stench of burnt skin and hair made me gag and cough. What the hell?

Angelica's mouth fell open. "Will, what are you doing?"

His shoulders slumped. He shook his head silently, then made a doorway, and disappeared.

The other four agents arrived, one by one. Realising the prisoner was dead, they all threw questions at once. But the only thing Angelica and I could do was look at each other.

There was nothing to say.

CHAPTER 16

L ate the following afternoon, after clearing the rest of the properties booked in for selling because of "ghosts," we pulled into the PIB car park. Fatigue was an understatement for the heavy drag on my body and mind. Last night, we'd magicked new windows into Mrs Soames's frames and cleaned the mess so it didn't look as if anything weird had happened. We'd magicked incense into the house and taken her over, telling her we'd cleared the ghost with smudge sticks.

She bought it.

This morning, we moved her back in—cockatoo, table, and all. It was a shame I couldn't enjoy the moment because of Will. It was clear he hadn't wanted to do what he'd done last night—he'd been forced. But by whom, and was he in more danger than he'd been able to let on? Our meeting would hopefully bring an action plan into being for how to extract him safely.

As we went up in the lift, Ma'am whispered a bubble-of-silence spell that included normal hearing too. "Go along with me in the meeting. I've invited a few extra agents. Act just as surprised and upset at the news as everyone else. Okay?"

"Of course." I gave her the most intense gaze I could. "You can always count on me." Hmm, what did she have up her witchy sleeve? It had better be good, or we may never see Will alive again. He'd lost control of the situation. We'd all underestimated this snake group. Maybe they'd been right to be cocky about their operation? I shivered and hugged myself, my chest tight with pent-up grief and fear.

Ma'am led the way into the conference room, which was good because I almost stopped and ran back out. Conversations rumbled through the room. The table was full, and extra chairs had been brought in to accommodate even more agents. What was she doing? Sitting at the table was one of the agents we suspected as being one of Dana's lackeys. Hmm.

Ma'am pulled her chair out and stood in front of it at the head of the table. Liv and James were sitting closest to her, but Beren and Imani were sitting amongst the plethora of black-suited agents. There was one empty seat, which just happened to be to Ma'am's right and out from the table a bit, as there wasn't room. She nodded to me and gestured to the seat. Crap.

I sat and clutched my bag in my lap, using it as a shield

against the stares. There was no table to protect me. Everyone was probably wondering what I was doing here, or maybe they thought I was one of them since I was wearing the uniform, but still, my lack of confidence probably screamed "imposter."

Telltale warmth spread across the back of my neck. A brass-coloured gong appeared in Ma'am's hand, a little metal hammer in the other. She hit it against the gong three times, and everyone fell quiet. Why was three such an oft-used number? When people raced, it was on three, when anyone wanted to countdown, it was from three. Why not four? What had four ever done to anyone? Although that was the Chinese word for death. Okay, so use five.

"I've called an emergency meeting today because we have a dire situation."

I focussed on Ma'am and pretended some of the agents weren't still staring at me. Apparently me being shocked and reactive was important to pulling this off—whatever *this* was.

"One of our agents has defected to a life of crime. He was working undercover, but it appears as though he's decided to join an organised-crime syndicate." Oh, so that's where she was going. "He's now a wanted man. Anyone with information as to his whereabouts is to let me know. If anyone hears from him, I want to be informed immediately. If found, he will be arrested and charged with murder. That agent's name is William Blakesley."

There were gasps and murmurs around the room. My gasp wasn't quite the loudest—I didn't want to overdo it and be obvious—but it was up there. My hand was plastered across my mouth. Some of these agents would know that we'd been an item... once. I let my tears come to the surface. I hated crying in front of people, but let them see how upset I was. I still wasn't sure where she was trying to lead everyone, but I would do whatever it took to get him back. God, how I wished we'd never sent him undercover. There had to be a better way to find out what happened to my parents. I couldn't risk any more people I loved. It wasn't worth it, was it?

Ma'am rang her gong once to quieten the chatter that was getting out of control. It wasn't often an agent defected, but when it happened, it was serious. Will knew many PIB secrets, and I imagined everyone was worried—well, everyone except that crappy agent who was probably on Dana's payroll. He sat there with a surprised expression, but as soon as he thought no one was watching him, his face went into poker mode. Even so, he nodded slowly, probably thinking about how well things were going. I turned my gaze away, not wanting him to catch me. I was close to narrowing my eyes in anger and giving myself away. This spying thing was way harder than it looked.

She was still standing and held up the gong, mallet poised to strike again. "Quiet please." Mouths closed, and heads turned her way. "This meeting was to advise you of the situation, but by no means do I want anyone to act on their own to apprehend him. I'm putting a small team together to find him and make an arrest. If we can't apprehend him, we will kill him if it looks like he's getting away. We have new information on the group he's defected to, and we're closing in on them, so any information William has may not be important anyway."

The bad-guy agent tried to keep his face neutral, but I saw the miniscule widening of his eyes. Ma'am opened her mouth to keep talking, and his hand went to his pocket and pulled out his phone. Hmm, had Ma'am spelled it? Was she looking for him to lead us to Will? "I'm going to call three names. The rest of you can go." She paused and surveyed the room. "Agent Bianchi." She gave my brother a side-eyed glance. "Agent Price." She looked down the table at the enemy agent. He smirked and nodded. Idiot. He probably thought he was being favoured above other agents. I was betting Ma'am had chosen him for a different reason. "And Agent Bradford." She stared at a guy in his thirties, whose straight dark hair was cut short, making his square jaw more pronounced. I had no idea if he was trustworthy or not, but like everything else she did, Ma'am would have her reasons.

Ma'am turned to Olivia and spoke loud enough that everyone exiting could probably still hear over the new chitchat. "Take Lily back to your office. Have her do some filing, please."

Olivia stood, the skin between her eyes furrowed. "Yes, Ma'am. I have a ton of that." My friend looked at me and jerked her head to the door. I sighed, trying to look as sad as possible, and joined her at the door. We exited together, bumping at the hip as we tried to fit through. A giggle bubbled to the surface, but I quickly schooled my face—I was supposed to be the grieving, disappointed ex-girlfriend. We hurried to her office and shut the door. Once we were safely inside, I made a bubble of total silence—it had taken me a while, but I'd finally come up with a new name for the spell that stopped every kind of listening in.

I sat in the chair next to Olivia's and twirled it around. Oops, bad idea. I was going to make myself sick. I stopped and looked at her as she sat. "Do you know what Ma'am's plan is? What if someone sees Will and decides to kill him for the PIB?"

"Don't worry. She's had James and Beren develop a spell. No one knows about it yet. It's groundbreaking and taps into telephone conversations and messages coming from any phone within one mile of this building. She's goaded that agent into acting. Ma'am made sure he'd make a phone call too—she put the suggestion in his mind. It's not legal, I know, but I'm sure we all agree this is one time we need to break the rules."

My eyes were wide. They were taking a lot of risks to save the man I cared about, and I couldn't thank them enough. More tears filled my eyes. "You don't have to convince me, Liv. This is all my fault. If we weren't trying to find out about my parents, none of this would have happened."

She shook her head. "Don't be silly. We still need to track down Dana, and this has a lot to do with her. And don't forget how many people that snake group has ripped off. This is bigger than your parents." She sank back into her chair.

She was right though. What happened to my parents was probably the tip of the iceberg. The longer this went on, the more I figured my parents must have been onto them too, trying to find a way to stop them. Obviously, they'd failed, and we appeared to be heading that way too. But it wasn't over yet.

I stood and went to the window. Twilight darkened the parklike grounds. Cold air radiated from the surface of the double-glazed windows. I shuddered, but it wasn't from that. "What if they kill him first? This plan could backfire."

Her chair creaked. She stood next to me, put her arm around my shoulders, and squeezed my upper arm. "Don't think about that. We'll get him back, and he'll be okay."

The sky faded to charcoal, turning the trees to nebulous shadows. He was out there, somewhere. The ache in my heart swelled, overflowing, sinking. I closed my eyes and placed my palms on the chilly glass. I pictured his tortured face from last night, his blue-grey eyes filled with pain. He probably wasn't upset about having to kill a criminal, but he would've known how it would hurt our chances of finding out more about my parents' disappearance and the snake group.

Wherever you are, Will, I love you. The words didn't shock me—I'd been trying not to think them for a while now, but it was true. And this wasn't the time I wanted to admit it to myself, but if not now, when? It might be too late anyway. I sent my love past the cold glass, outside into the descending night, hoping it would find its mark. If only he knew, maybe it would give him comfort. I didn't want him to die without knowing.

I didn't want him to die.

My stomach hummed with the comforting warmth of the river of magic. It filtered up to heat my glass-cooled fingertips. Then it was flowing outwards, and I let it. Even though it made me sleepy, the flow was reassuring, connecting me to the source, to life.

Lily, you have to get out of my mind. They stripped my mind-shield. Any of them could be listening.

My eyes sprang open. What the hell? I shut my eyes again. *Will?*

His presence, despite the skittish undercurrent of fear and pain, enveloped me reassuringly. My bones absorbed the solace as if it were life-saving water to a parched desert. *Where are you?*

Don't come. It's booby-trapped. I'll figure it out.

Sharp pain flared in my chest, and the heat of his essence withdrew. The river flowing from my fingers stopped.

He was gone.

I opened my eyes again to Oliva's face in front of mine, her pointer finger tapping the end of my nose. She jerked back. "Oh my God. What happened? Where did you go? I was talking to you, but you didn't answer. You wouldn't respond to me tapping your face either." She put her hand on her chest. "I thought you'd taken a weird turn from when you almost died."

"I'm fine… well, not *fine*, fine." I checked that the bubble of total silence was still up. Yep. "I'm not quite sure I believe what just happened, but I contacted Will." *And he's in pain.*

Panic flared, blocking my throat, preventing me from speaking.

Her brow wrinkled, and her eyes squinted. "But you don't have your phone out."

I couldn't blame her for not getting it—even though I'd done it, I still didn't understand what I'd really done. "I was missing him like hell, and I thought about him. My magic decided to go wandering, and it found him. His voice was in my mind, and he heard my thoughts too."

"No way!" She peered into my eyes, then put her hand on my forehead.

I rolled my eyes and shook her hand off. "I don't have a temperature. Seriously. I'm not sick or crazy." I crossed my fingers behind my back. What if I was crazy, and I'd only *thought* he was talking to me because I wanted it so much. But feeling him there with me… it had been such a strong, intense sensation. It had to be real. "Oh, crap. We have to tell Ma'am." I grabbed my phone out of my bag and dialled her. It went to voicemail. I hung up. I didn't trust this to a message. She was probably still in that meeting with the chosen few.

"Ma'am's going to think you're as crazy as I do. Why is it so urgent?"

"He had a message, and like I said, I could feel his pain. They've booby-trapped the place he's in." It hit me what a funny expression that was. If we weren't in such a dire situation, I'd laugh at the image of detached boobs flying around hitting people, knocking them out. Maybe I *was* crazy….

Her eyes widened. "If you're right, she needs to know."

I clamped my mouth shut against the "ya think" that almost came out. She couldn't be blamed for not believing me. As far as I knew, no one had done that before, and why should I be so special as to have a skill no one else had? Yes, my witchy photography skills were unique, but that just meant there was even less of a chance that I should have another special talent. "She definitely needs to know." We looked at each other and nodded. I smiled, and she glanced at the door. She was obviously thinking the same thing as me. We ran to the door and out to the hallway before sprinting to the conference room.

Gus was standing outside, presumably guarding the door to make sure someone didn't just barge in. Damn. "Hey, Gus!" I smiled.

"Hello, Miss Lily, Miss Olivia. What can I do you for?"

I dropped my happy expression, replacing it with a grave one. This was urgent, and I didn't have time to try and manipulate my way in. To be honest, with Gus, I probably didn't need to. "We need to speak to Ma'am right now. It's super urgent and has something to do with what's going on in there."

He drew his brows together. "I'm afraid that's impossible."

Gah, why did Gus have to go and get all difficult on me? Normally he was the epitome of helpful. "But you don't understand. It's life or death. We have to tell her something highly classified."

He shook his head. "I'd help you if I could, but she's not

WITCH HAUNTED IN WESTERHAM

in there. She and her agents left a couple of minutes ago. There's a different meeting in there now."

My stomach free-fell. "Ah, thanks, Gus."

"Are you okay, Miss Lily? You don't look too well."

Yep, that would be because there was no blood left in my face. What the hell were we going to do now? "I'll be okay… maybe. Thanks anyway. We have to get going. Bye."

"Good luck." He shrugged, maybe in apology—who knew.

I grabbed Olivia's hand and dragged her back to her office. Once inside, I called James. When it went to voicemail, I growled. My thoughts raced but got nowhere as I discarded one idea after another. We had no idea where they were headed, and I didn't know how to track them. Surely there was some kind of backup system in case something bad happened. I turned to Olivia. "Do you know if Ma'am would've told anyone where they were going, you know, just in case it all went pear-shaped? I mean, they may not have gone running after Will yet, right?"

"If Agent Price contacted someone straight away, they would've gotten on it. I can't see Ma'am wasting any time getting to Will. Can you?"

"No. If they had gone to find Will, would they even take Price with them? Wouldn't that mean they would have to watch out for him too?"

She nodded. "Maybe call Millicent. If anyone would know, it's her. Even though James keeps things confidential, I have a feeling he'd tell her—she's his second in command, after all."

Before I went to James's house, I called Imani. "Hey, I need you."

"Where and when?"

I smiled. I knew she'd have my back. "Meet me at James's now."

"Done. Bye."

I grabbed Liv's hand. "Ready?"

She nodded. I made my doorway, and we stepped through. I actually had no idea if she'd be at home—I probably should've checked. As I knocked on the door, Imani appeared behind us. "Hi, ladies."

We both said, "Hi."

Millicent said, "Who's there?"

I breathed out, unbelievably relieved. "It's me, Lily. I've got Liv and Imani with me."

The door opened. Millicent had one hand on her belly. She wasn't smiling. "What's wrong?"

I created a bubble of silence. "Where have Ma'am and James gone? I contacted Will. Wherever he's being kept, there're traps. They're waiting for them."

She blinked. "What do you mean, you've contacted Will?"

"Yes, Lily. How?" Imani added.

Gah, this was time wasting. "I don't know exactly how, but I was thinking about him, and my magic kind of took over. We had a small chat, mind to mind, but he couldn't say too much because they forced him to take down his mind-shield."

Millicent's mouth dropped open. Imani moved in front

of me, grabbed both my shoulders, and stared into my eyes. "Do you realise how incredible that is? I shouldn't be surprised because I already knew you were special, but this is…." She shook her head.

"Thanks, but we don't have time for this right now. I'll bask in the praise later." At least they believed me. "What can we do? I think Ma'am and James have already left to get him."

"They're already expecting there will be problems, Lily. They let Agent Price contact his people, don't forget. They had to, to find out where they were holding Will. As soon as they got that information, they chucked Agent Price in a PIB cell." That was huge news. Up till now, most of the people who'd had contact with the snake group had been killed. We hadn't been able to get information out of anyone. And phew that the extra threat of Agent Price was out of the way.

"Yes, I get they'd already be expecting trouble, but Will said the place he's in has been booby-trapped, and I know how you guys operate. You're careful, but these traps were in place before they knew the PIB was coming for Will today. Maybe this is part of a greater plan? If they take out James, Will, and, Ma'am, it won't just destroy us personally —the PIB will be a disaster." Ma'am shouldn't have gone. She probably only went because it was Will. My headache returned, pounding against my temples with ferocious intent. "Imani and I need to go as backup. It's the only way to keep it private, and we won't let anyone know we're there unless we need to step in. Maybe you can mobilise a team without telling them what they'll be doing, and if we need them, we'll call. If it gets to that point, we have nothing to lose anyway. Surely there's protocol for this sort of thing?"

Millicent worried her bottom lip between her teeth. "Come in." She stepped aside, and we walked through to the dining room, where we normally had our snake-group meetings. But I didn't sit—I was too worked up. We needed to get moving.

"We don't have time to chat. We have to go."

"I'm not telling you where they went until we go through a plan. I'm not putting you and Imani in needless danger. We're doing this my way or no way at all." She raised a brow and put her hands on her hips. "Now sit for two minutes while we get this sorted."

Wow, Millicent could be bossy when she wanted to be. I sat. Millicent sat next to me, while Imani and Olivia sat across from us. Imani looked at Mill. "Carter, Frank, Knight, and Smith. I trust them implicitly, and they've got a hell of a lot of experience."

Mill nodded. "Yes, I'd agree with that assessment. Okay, so we have the agents. I'll check they're not assigned to something I can't pull them out of on short notice." An iPad thingy appeared on the table in front of her. It looked like the one PIB security had started using. She typed stuff in, waited for information to load, and searched. I pulled my phone out and checked the time. Tick, tick, tick. My leg bounced manically under the table. Soon, my transformation to a squirrel would be complete. If only. I'd bet there were no squirrels having to send out a search-and-save party for someone they loved. All they worried about were nuts. Why, then, were they always so nervous? Maybe they had a little world we knew nothing about. They *were* secretive little things. Hmm. They'd make a good army of spies. The PIB should really look into it. I could be queen of the super-secret-squirrel spy bureau. They could have little uniforms with SSSSB on the front.

"Lily? Lily!" Millicent waved a hand across my face, and I started.

Gah, I'd tuned out by accident. Imani frowned. I shrugged. "Sorry. I'm back. Do we have a plan?" And, yes, I realised I'd just wasted valuable time.

Millicent looked at the ceiling, likely asking the universe *why me.* "Those agents are all available. I've sent them a classified message to be on standby for the next sixty minutes. If we need them, we'll know by then. And Beren's on standby in case of injuries. Here." She held out her hand, and something appeared in her palm. "I don't trust you with a gun— you've had no training—but if for some reason you need a weapon and you don't have your magic, this is a Taser. Just flick the safety off, point it at the person you want to zap, and push this button."

I carefully took it from her, looked at it to make sure I knew where all the buttons were, then slipped it into my inside jacket pocket. "Thanks. And, yeah, I'm not ready for a gun."

Imani cocked her head and regarded me. She nodded slowly, appearing to come to a conclusion—about what, I had no idea. "We're to stay out of sight—we're observers, Lily. Understand?"

Sheesh, now Imani was on my case too. "Yes, definitely. I have no intention of doing something stupid and putting anyone in danger. We'll watch, and if we think Ma'am and James need it, we'll call for support."

Millicent rubbed her tummy again. "That's good, Lily. That's exactly what you're going to do. And Imani is the professional in this situation, so you have to do whatever she tells you as soon as she tells you. No arguments. Understood?"

Gah, there she went, laying down the law. "You know you sound just like Ma'am." I looked at her tummy. "When the baby decides to run away, he or she can come live with Auntie Lily where no one will boss anyone around and make them promise stuff that's nearly impossible to comply with."

She rolled her eyes. "Goddammit, Lily. Can you take this seriously?"

"I *am* taking it seriously. But how many times have I had to do something against orders, and it turned out it was the best thing for me to do? I can't change who I am, Mill. If I have to break a rule to save someone I love, I'm going to do it every single time." I was an idiot for being honest because I didn't want to get banned from going, but it was the elephant in the room. Why did they keep expecting the impossible from me? They needed to give up on expecting me to blindly obey.

Millicent huffed, but she didn't argue. "Just be careful." She shook her head. "If anything happens to you on my watch, James will never speak to me again, and our baby will have divorced parents."

Oh, I hadn't thought of that—she felt responsible for me. "I'll behave, okay? Besides, this isn't your fault. You know something has to be done, and I want to do it. I promise to come back alive. Okay?"

"I'll hold you to that." She grabbed my hand and squeezed it. "Seriously, be careful."

I nodded. "Promise." I looked at Imani. "Ready?"

"Yep. I'll make the doorway for both of us."

Millicent spoke. "They're at an empty factory an hour from here. We have a cubicle a five-minute walk from there. Here are the coordinates." She must have only sent them to Imani because no golden numbers appeared in my mind. She released my hand and stood. "Good luck, ladies."

Olivia stood, gave Imani a hug, and came around the table, giving me a hug when I stood. "Watch out for each other. Okay? And come back safe."

I squeezed her and let my hands fall. "I will." I glanced at Imani. "We both will." I quirked up one corner of my mouth in an abysmal attempt at a smile. "See you later tonight."

I moved away from the table, and Imani joined me. She made her doorway and grabbed my hand. As we walked through, I whispered, "We're coming, Will. Hold on."

CHAPTER 17

The public toilet we'd been sent to stunk. It was grimy and ancient, and we pushed and shoved each other in our attempt to be the first out of there. It took the whole walk to the factory to banish the stench from my nostrils. Fifty metres from the site, mesh fencing came into view under streetlights. Barbed wire ringed the top of it, and the three-metre-high gate was closed. We stopped and crouched, taking a minute to check it out and think about what our next move should be. Surprise was on our side, and we didn't want to do anything to jeopardise our only advantage.

Imani whispered, "Is your return-to-sender up?"

I made it, then answered, "It is now." It was important to get that stuff sorted now so no one would sense our magic. We were far enough from the factory that our small use of magic would go undetected. "How are we going to get in? What if they've got video cameras around the place?"

"I have no doubt they do. We'll just find where Ma'am went in. They would've dealt with the cameras already."

"What about the traps. Is there a detection spell we can use?"

"Yes, but whoever's there will feel that someone is using magic. It'll give us away."

"But they're already expecting Ma'am and some agents. No one knows we're here, so the snake group will think it's Ma'am, and Ma'am will think it's them. We can use that for cover."

"That could actually work."

I smiled. "The only other option is disappearing the factory so everything inside is exposed, and I doubt we have enough power for that."

Imani sniggered. "Ah, yeah. Your deduction is correct." She pulled a gun from a holster under her jacket. "We'll find a way in. Follow me. Stop when I stop, take cover if I take cover, etcetera. Don't do anything unless I say. Don't go anywhere unless you're following me, or I tell you to. Understood?"

"Yes." She needed to keep her mind on the job without worrying about what stupidity I was going to unleash. At this stage, I planned on doing as I was told.

She ran towards the factory, hunched over like you see in the movies, so I did the same. It was a dangerous game of follow-the-leader. Our footfalls seemed to thunder and echo in the quiet night. The frigid air sawed in and out of my throat, pluming white in front of my face when we halted to check out a gap in the wire further along the street.

Without a word, Imani approached the fence and slipped through a hole that had been cut out of it. The factory was about fifty metres further into the block, but three industrial-sized metal bins stood to our right. Imani sprinted to them and hid behind one. I crouched next to her and listened. There was no sound. I was taking that as a good sign—no one had confronted anyone yet. We were hopefully in time.

"Now what?" I whispered. Even though everything seemed to be peaceful, Will was in there somewhere, at the mercy of a group who hated us, and they were hurting him.

"We'll move closer to the factory and find where they went in. It's risky, but that's all we can do."

"Hey, why don't I just take a photo?" I stood and slid my phone out of my back pocket. The magic I used with my talent was mainly from my own reserves, so it shouldn't be enough for anyone else to feel. "Show me where Ma'am went into the factory." I leaned out from the cover of the bin and pointed my phone camera at the massive rundown building. Hmm. I ducked back behind the bin. "Nothing. They must have gone in around the back or the other side that I can't see from here. Why don't we pop out over there and hug the fence line? The row of trees should be fairly good cover." I pointed to the fence that was to the right as you faced the property. A line of pines followed that boundary and blocked some of the light from the street. The only other illumination was in the actual factory—a yellow glow came from two windows on the second floor. The rest of the grounds were shadowy and indistinct.

"Okay. No mucking around. Let's go." She jumped up and ran for the fence, me at her heels. When we were about ten metres from the factory, Imani put her back against one of the trunks and held her gun at the ready as she surveyed the factory. She gave me a quick nod. I pointed my phone at the factory and whispered, "Show me where Ma'am entered the building." Thank God. There she was at a door near the back of the factory. James must have already gone in because there was only one other person with her, unless my brother had gone in a different way. "Show me James entering the building." Nothing. So he had gone in some-where else. I swallowed my concern—worrying about it now would only divert my attention from where it needed to be.

I leaned close to Imani's ear. I didn't want to show her the photo, as the light might give us away. "She went in that door there, near the corner. But James didn't go in that one. I don't know where he entered. Should we split up too?"

She shook her head. "No way. You don't leave my sight."

I let the statement roll over my head. I wasn't a trained agent, but it still stung that everyone thought I was helpless. Whatever. *Get over yourself, Lily. This isn't about you.* While I was having a pity party, Imani set off, and I had to sprint to catch her. She was staying along the boundary. She halted without warning, and I did my best to stop but ended up ploughing into her. We both stumbled but managed not to lose our footing. She frowned at me. I shrugged. Neither of us wanted to speak in case someone heard. The less we talked, the better.

I lifted my phone and pointed it at the other side of the factory, which was visible from our new vantage point. I quietly said, "Show me where James entered the building. Crap." Far down the other end of the building, a dark figure held tight to something on the wall with one hand and his legs as he leaned across to grab the second-storey window frame with the other hand. My mouth close to Imani's ear, I murmured, "Top floor, far window." She nodded.

What would she decide? I wasn't in any condition to climb buildings like Spiderman, and we couldn't use magic. I had no doubt that Imani was capable of the climb though. "You should go through the window. I'll go through the door. I know you didn't want to split up, but maybe we should."

"No. How many times do I have to say it?"

A shockwave—there was no other way to describe it—of power came from the factory, knocking both of us to the ground. I hit the ground bottom first and rolled backwards, ending up facing the factory on my knees. Geez that hurt. I rubbed my bum. Imani was rising after landing on her back. We looked at each other. "What the hell was that?"

Her eyes were wide. "I have no idea, but we need to get in there." She didn't have to tell me twice. We ran for the door Ma'am had gone in. I pulled out my Taser, just in case, but now that the hum of magic thrummed over my scalp, we could use ours too, and no one would be the wiser.

All the lights had gone out when the explosion of power

happened, so when we silently entered, we did so into inky blackness. Stale dust and the thick stench of oil coated my nostrils. The ancient mechanic's shop my dad used to take his car to had smelt like this. My pulse hammered loudly in my ears until it was drowned out by yelling that came from whoever was beyond the room we'd entered. I put my hand on Imani's shoulder so I wouldn't lose her. She felt her way through the space, and I stuck my hand out too, feeling a table and wooden boxes as we went. Based on the noise, the next doorway was straight ahead.

Imani reached it and stopped. We both listened, and I didn't know about her, but I held my breath, desperate for as much information as possible before we stumbled blindly into the fray. Imani held her gun out in front with both hands. I didn't know how effective that was, or even safe since our friends were in there, and we couldn't see a damned thing. If I tried to contact Will again, surely no one would be able to tell where I was. Maybe I could pretend to be far from there. But it took a fair bit of magic to do what I'd done before, and could I even replicate it? It'd kind of been an unconscious thing.

Imani moved forward one slow step at a time. I could sense objects to my left and right. A cold breath of air puffed over my face, and I flinched. There was space in front of us, but anything could come out of it at any time. Being blind was not my favourite thing. Goosebumps slithered over my arms. I ran my hand down Imani's arm, letting her know I was going to crawl the rest of the way. The vulnerability of walking unseeing was too much, and if the lights did suddenly come on, I wouldn't be as visible down low. Imani must have agreed because she dropped down next to me.

"Give it up, DuPree. This is one battle you can't win. If you don't leave now, we'll kill him. Better to leave him with us and save yourself. This is the last offer you'll get. Stay, and we'll kill you and your two agents, but we'll leave William alive—the boss isn't finished with him yet." The man laughed. The voice was coming from somewhere in front of us, and high up. Ma'am stayed silent, not falling for his threat, not that I'd expected her to.

Something scraped to my left. A flash and loud crack followed by darkness. It left a negative of the area in my eyes. Box shapes, which I was going to assume were stacked boxes, an old car, and clutter. High on what might be a walkway, where you'd expect a ceiling to be, was a figure. They would have been concentrating on wherever that shot of lightning had gone and wouldn't have seen us—thank God we were on the floor. I had to wonder why he cast a spell when everyone likely had their return-to-sender spells activated. Maybe this guy thought he was stronger than everyone else? I shuddered. Maybe he was.

A screamed echoed from somewhere further into the building. The man spoke again. "Hear that? The longer you stay, the more William will suffer. We'll be careful to keep him alive, as I've said, because where would the fun be in torturing a dead body?"

My heart constricted, and my lungs seized. *Will.* What were Ma'am and James doing? Why was it taking so long?

From what I could hear, there were two bad guys in here—the one talking, and the one torturing.

A scream filled the place again, and I started crawling towards it. Imani grabbed my ankle, stopping me from going further. She squeezed hard. I stopped, pretending I'd gotten the message that I was not allowed to move. As soon as she released her grip, I'd be off.

"Okay. We're going." Ma'am from behind us. Was she at the door? And where were James and the other agent? They couldn't be giving up. Knowing them, they definitely had a plan to get Will out of here, and they were buying time.

"Let me hear your other two agents. I wasn't born yesterday." The man's voice had moved—he was still up high but to my right. If only Imani would get her hand off my ankle. I sat back, forcing her to move her hand or have it squashed by my bottom. She complied. I was also hoping she'd think I'd given up on the idea of going anywhere.

"I'm here." James.

"So am I." The other guy.

"If you hurt Agent Blakesley after we leave, we'll bring every agent we have to destroy this place. We'll hunt you and your friends down and lock you up for eternity." Oh my God, Ma'am really sounded like she was giving up. But surely she couldn't be. It was her job to be convincing, to have the goal in focus. Even if she wanted to stay and get Will, it wasn't going to be easy. Imani and I would have to play our part.

A raw-throated howl from Will twisted my stomach, leaving me wrung out. The man's matter-of-fact tone made me want to strangle him. "Just a reminder what awaits our beloved William if you stay. For every minute you're here, we'll give him another moment of pain. How many more will you force him to suffer?"

Jesus, these guys were evil. My breath came faster, and anger waltzed with fear, enlivening my blood. This was unacceptable. If I had to listen to him being tortured again, I'd throw up.

"We're leaving," Ma'am called from behind us. Her retreating footsteps were joined by two other people, who must be James and the other agent. The guy on the rafter-space walkway chuckled. There was something sinister in that understated show of mirth.

My mouth dropped open. "No!" I screamed and jumped up.

But I was too late.

The room we'd originally entered, the room Ma'am and my brother were in, exploded. I was thrown backwards and slammed into a solid stack of something, probably timber crates. Pain erupted through my skull on impact. I groaned and ran my fingers over my scalp. No blood. Good.

Orange light flickered and glowed, colouring my skin. I yelled to Imani. "Save them."

She was stumbling to her feet. Our eyes met, and she nodded, her face set with determination. I spun around and looked up. The fiery luminescence bathed the empty walk-way. Damn. He'd gone. As soon as he or his accomplice grabbed Will, they could leave via a doorway, and we'd never see him again. I opened the portal to the river of power and drew it in, till I was bursting with it, my veins almost crackling like the fire behind me.

"Witches travel via magical doorways. All such doorways in this building lead to me for the next five minutes." My magic shot out and swirled around. I couldn't see it, but I could sense it the same way I sensed Will this afternoon. I stood with my back against the crates, Taser poised. I was torn between running around to find Will or waiting for them to turn up here—surely their first instinct would be to leave. If they didn't turn up in another sixty seconds, I would go and find Will.

A splash, sizzle, and hiss came from the fire. Imani was magicking a fountain of water on it. Would Ma'am and James be okay? I stared at the doorway, trying not to cry or run towards them. I had to stay the course here. If I tried to help, I might miss saving Will, and maybe lose everyone.

The river of power surged within me, gushing out of my hands. My legs became heavy, jellylike. I pressed my back against the boxes, refusing to sink to the ground. I flicked the safety off and held the Taser out.

Will was shoved out of the air in front of me. His eyes widened when he saw me. He let whoever was behind him keep pushing forward. I held up the Taser and jerked my head to the side, indicating he needed to get out of the other guy's grip as soon as he could.

When the man came out of his doorway, Will fell forward, out of his grip. The man saw me, maybe realised where he was, and he stopped and flung his hands up, probably about to cast a spell. That was my cue. I pressed the

Taser button and fired. The wires shot out and hit his throat. His eyes shot open, and his shriek came from a convulsing body. He collapsed, rigid and shaking.

I quickly checked his aura. Any spells he may have been holding onto were gone. I smiled. Looked as if Tasers were good for shocking spells from witches. I imagined the man falling asleep, then drew power and sent it towards him. "Make him sleep for ten minutes." It was wise to put a time limit on it, or I could possibly send him to sleep for years, although that would probably take more magic than I had. His eyes shut, and I breathed out a rush of relief. One problem down, one to go. I was about to turn to see if Will was okay, when he limped past me to Imani. He must have known what was in there.

I pressed my lips together and blinked tears back. *Please be okay.* I hurried to where Imani had just been before she disappeared through the doorway into smoky haze. The flames were gone at least. The only way Ma'am and James would still be okay is if they'd managed to throw up some kind of protection spell before they'd been overcome. I didn't like those chances though. I mean, there was no way they could have been ready for the explosion. Maybe they'd been knocked out before they could do anything.

I walked into the smoke. My burning eyes watered, and not just from the acrid haze. I coughed, closed my mouth, and pressed my arm against my nose. It was impossible to see anything. I stopped and steadied myself. Drawing one more pulse of power, I imagined a gust of wind blowing through the room and clearing the smoke. A wave of fatigue hit me the same time as the breeze.

My wobbly legs threatened to collapse. *Not now, damn you.* I breathed the fresher air, but now the fire was out, darkness had taken over again, and I couldn't see anything.

A ball of light winked into life next to me. "Lily?" Will croaked out.

I smiled as my eyes filled with new tears. "Where're Ma'am and James?"

"Imani found James. She's dragged him out. Ma'am was blown clear. She's outside, unconscious but alive. Beren's on his way. Imani's making a temporary landing zone."

"That guy who had you. He's asleep inside, but only for a few more minutes."

"Okay. I'll deal with him." He hurried outside and returned shortly, a pair of PIB cuffs in hand. He smiled at me as he passed on his way to the bastard on the floor in the factory.

I moved to the door and watched Will handcuff the guy, who was still asleep. I didn't want to let Will out of my sight now. Surely we didn't still have to pretend to be apart anymore. His cover was well and truly blown.

Someone groaned. Oh my God, the other agent! I turned and followed the sound. Only a skerrick of Will's light made it in here, so I hadn't noticed him before. He lay slumped against the wall. It was too dark to tell, but it looked as if his face was covered in blood. God, the poor man. I steeled my tired body and hooked my hands under his armpits and dragged him outside, through a hole that was much larger than the original doorway. That had been a powerful explosion.

Just as I'd crossed the threshold, Will found me. "Here, let me." I tried to protest, but he easily bumped me out of the way. I found where James lay, and I made my way to him and plonked onto the ground, exhausted. His eyes were closed, face blackened with soot. "James, can you hear me?"

His eyes slowly opened. "Lily?" He sounded confused, and he probably should have. Imani and I had managed to keep our presence a secret.

"I'm here. Where does it hurt?" I grabbed his hand and held it whilst trying to see where he was injured.

"My head hurts, my leg." He shifted and cried out. "Shit. I think it's broken."

"Beren's on his way. You'll be okay. I promise."

His jaw bulged as he gritted his teeth. He eventually relaxed enough to suck in a shallow breath. "But what are you doing here?"

"Imani and I snuck in, but I'll tell you later. We're both okay, and Will's out, alive."

"What about Ma'am?"

I looked over to where Imani sat. Ma'am was lying on the ground, her head on Imani's lap. "I'm not sure. She looks about as bad as you." I called out, "Imani. How's Ma'am?"

"She's alive." And that was the extent of her response.

I looked over at the other agent, who Will had dragged outside. Beren stepped through his doorway at the same time. He looked from Ma'am to James to the other agent and went straight to the other agent. He did look to be in a bad way—burnt, unconscious. James was injured, but I didn't think he was burnt.

Will finally came outside again, the snake guy slumped over his shoulder. Ten minutes was a long time in a disaster. It felt as if I'd put him to sleep an hour ago. Will's weary steps continued till he reached James and me. "I'm taking this guy back to the cells." I frowned. He'd lost weight, and there were dark shadows under his eyes. His haunted gaze wasn't what I was used to. What had they done to him? I wanted to jump up and hug the hell out of him, but James needed me, and Will had an armful of bad guy. "Lily, we'll catch up tomorrow. Okay?"

I nodded but couldn't speak, lest I bawl like a big baby. Were we good, or had too much happened? Was he even okay? James, even in his broken state, squeezed my hand. He knew me, knew I was heartsore.

Will offered me a lacklustre half smile before disappearing through his doorway.

It was going to be a long night.

CHAPTER 18

I yawned as I sipped my morning coffee at the kitchen table, although eleven forty-five only *just* qualified as morning. Last night, I'd showered, then dropped into bed at 1:00 a.m. Despite the craziness, violence, and my apprehension about the conversation Will and I were going to have, I fell asleep straight away. The exhaustion of using so much magic was the perfect antidote to insomnia. Beren had healed Angelica and brought her home, magicking her clean and putting her to bed. I didn't blame him for not wanting to help shower her the normal way. He would have copped an earful when she woke up. Maybe he should have showered her—it would have given me something to laugh about later when he was under fire.

I'd checked on her ten minutes ago, when I'd gotten up. She'd smiled and said she was going to get ready soon and to meet her at the PIB for a 1:30 p.m. meeting. At least she was giving everyone time to sleep in. I doubted any of us were feeling like doing much today. Olivia had gone to work at the usual time this morning, but I didn't hear her go, and yay that Ethel was back at her home across the road. If solving this case did nothing else, it got us our home back from the noisy, annoying clutches of our neighbour and her bird. And, hey, I should have felt an affinity for the bird since it originated from my home country, but nuh-uh. Anything that woke me up with ear-splitting, prehistoric cries at five in the morning was a big, fat nope.

When my coffee was done, I donned my boots and coat, wandered across the road, and knocked on Mrs Soames's door—no, I didn't miss her already, but I needed to know if her home remained clear of paranormal activity. She answered the door, Ethel on her shoulder, and even managed a smile. That was my answer. "Oh, Lily. How are you? You look a little tired, actually."

Ha ha, thanks. "I'm good, thank you. I just came by to see how you were doing. Is everything as it should be?" I was pretty sure I didn't need to elaborate on what I meant.

She stroked Ethel's head. "Yes, thank you. You and Angelica did a wonderful job. There's been nothing but peace and quiet since I moved back in."

"Peace and quiet, rawrk! Peace and quiet, rawrk!"

I laughed. There was nothing peaceful or quiet about that bird. "Great to hear. If you need anything else, let us know."

"I think you've done more than enough. Thanks again." Ethel bobbed up and down, as if agreeing.

I smiled. Okay, so she'd been super irritating, but I was genuinely pleased she was enjoying her home again, and not just because it got her out of our hair. It was nice to see her happy. "It was our pleasure. See you later." Funny expression, that. I'd often used it as a way of saying goodbye to people I knew I would never see again—like the stranger you're introduced to on the job, or at a party. *Meh.* I shrugged. People were weird, so it was only natural that our language reflected it. I turned and went home.

As soon as I was in the front door, I travelled to the PIB reception room—I didn't feel like moping around alone until the meeting. Olivia was at the PIB this week, so I'd duck in and say hello. Gus wasn't there, but neither was that evil woman because she got fired. *Sucked in.* It was a young guy, about my age, with close-shaven dark hair, dark skin, and large brown eyes. He held out the device. "Hello, Miss. Can I ask you to place your palm here, please?"

I plonked my hand on it.

"Please state your name and address."

"Lily Bianchi." I gave him Angelica's address.

"Excellent. Thank you." He lowered the device and smiled. "And who are you here to see today?"

"Olivia. She works for Millicent Bianchi."

"Oh, are you and Millicent related, then?"

I grinned. "She's my sister-in-law."

His eyes widened. "Oh, cool. Your brother's high up here."

"That he is."

"Well, I won't keep you any longer. Lovely to meet you, Lily. Have a wonderful day."

"Thanks! You too." I set off for Millicent's office a little bit happier. It didn't take much to be nice, and what a difference it could make to someone's day. That guard had been super friendly. Why couldn't everyone be like that?

When I walked into the office, Olivia was sitting in her chair, Millicent was in hers, and Imani was perched on Liv's desk. "Hey, having a get together without me? What gives?"

Liv jumped up and hurried over to give me a hug. "I'm so glad you're all right." She stood back and looked at me.

I smiled. "I'm fine."

Millicent stayed in her chair—I didn't blame her with the baby weighing her down. "We're relieved to see that. After almost losing your powers and being unwell, we weren't sure how you'd pull up today."

"A bit tired, but generally good." I sat in one of the chairs in front of Millicent's desk. "How are you feeling today, Imani? That waterfall was incredible." I hadn't had a chance to marvel at it last night with everything that had been going on.

She grinned. "I'm good. I didn't use nearly as much power as you, missy. You have a lot of explaining to do at the meeting."

I tensed my forehead. "What do you mean? Am I in trouble?" I sighed. I was so sick of being in trouble.

She laughed. "No, silly. Yet again, you did some incredible stuff, and we want to know how you did it."

"Oh, okay then." I relaxed my shoulders and sat back.

"Um, does anyone know how Will is? He looked pretty wrecked last night."

Millicent frowned. "He's as well as can be expected, but he's off duty for another week. Angelica called a little while ago and insisted."

Liv sat down. "Beren spent time with him last night, healed his wounds. He said he'll be okay… eventually. He's been through a lot, Lil. More than even he could have envisaged."

And that's what I'd been afraid of. "We'll help him get through it. No matter what." I blinked back tears. "Even if he doesn't want to get back to where we were, I'll be there for him as a friend." I shook my head. What horrible experiences lived behind his haunted gaze? Fury and a desire for revenge simmered in my gut. I clenched my fists until my fingers ached. Regula Pythonissam would pay, and Dana would pay the highest price of all. I'd make sure of it.

"Lily? Hello?" Imani eyeballed me, concern on her face.

I took a deep breath and calmed myself. "It's all good. So, who wants cake?" Changing the subject—my forte. I ordered cake, coffee, and tea from the cafeteria, and we talked about the weather, squirrels, and how nice the new guard was until it was time to move to the conference room.

Millicent and Olivia led the way, chatting about the baby's nursery and what was left to do. I followed with Imani, but I was no longer in the mood to talk. All I could think about was Will. Whatever happened, I would suck it up and move on. He didn't need the guilt of my heartbreak on top of everything else he'd been through. Losing him as a boyfriend was horrible, but losing him altogether would be even worse. And for the people who said there was one perfect person for everyone, I had to disagree for my own sanity. I'd felt Will was the one, and if a few weeks of bliss in the love department was the only happy relationship I'd ever have, what was the point?

Ma'am sat at the head of the table, her hair in an impeccable bun, her tie blacker than the darkest night. Her straight posture and alert gaze belied the fact that she was tired. The bags under her eyes gave her away. My brother, also looking worn but impeccable, sat to her left. Millicent took her place next to him, awkwardly settling into her chair. That baby needed to come out soon.

Beren sat to Ma'am's right. Olivia sat next to him. Imani dropped into the chair next to Millicent. There was a space next to Olivia, then Will with his back to me, and at the foot of the table, Agent Bradford, his square jaw still pronounced and sporting a scar. I'd thought Beren could erase scars. Maybe it took more than one healing? Or maybe Agent Bradford wanted a reminder of what he'd been through. Or maybe he believed the hype that chicks digged scars. My mouth quirked up on one side.

I carefully sat between Liv and Will. I looked at him. He turned his head and gave me a small smile. His eyes were battleship-grey today, and even though they spoke of suffering, somewhere deep inside, a spark of blue shone. It would take a while, but he would be okay. He had to be. "Hey, Lily."

My smile was tentative. "Hey, yourself. How are you feeling today?"

"I've been better, but I'm here."

"Whatever happens, I'm glad." I brightened my smile to show him I meant what I said.

He opened his mouth to respond, but Ma'am clapped her hands. I jumped and gasped. Bloody hell. When was I going to stop being so highly strung? Olivia chuckled. Yeah, very funny.

"Let's get this meeting underway; then we can all go home and get some rest. Firstly, I'll get the bad news out of the way." *Bad news?* Wasn't this meant to be a recap and a how-to-move-forward meeting? "As you know, we put Agent Price in lockup yesterday before we left. The guards who went in to give him breakfast this morning found his body. They then checked the cell where we placed the man from last night. He's also dead. We're autopsying the bodies, but the results won't be in for a few days. We're going to have to do this as thoroughly as possible, think of every angle."

Crap. This stupid snake group was leaving us with nothing. Abso-bloody-lutely nothing. Beren gazed at Will, but I had no idea what he was thinking. His poker face was almost as good as his aunt's when he wanted it to be.

Ma'am continued. "Over the next few days, Will's going to provide as many details as he can. He's started his report, which will remain classified. I'll let you all know the details I believe you need to know. After last night, Agent Bradford will be helping James and me with our investigations into this criminal group of witches. The fact those two men were murdered in our cells without anyone noticing until it was too late is cause for concern. We have to ferret out all the rats in this organisation."

Crap. That's why Beren was looking at Will. He had more information on these people than anyone we had access to. The sooner he relayed that information, the better. If they couldn't kill him within the next few days, they'd be wasting time and energy trying to get to him. How much danger was he in right now?

James interrupted. "Because of this, Will, we're putting you in hiding after this meeting."

Will cocked his head to the side. "With all due respect, James, Ma'am, you don't need to do that. My home is well protected. I can take care of myself."

Ever the guy. Why couldn't men accept help when they needed it? I narrowed my eyes and gave him my laser-eyed stare. "I hate to be the one to say it, but what about last night? What would've happened to you if we hadn't turned up?" His eyes darkened, his pupils dilating, ready for an argument. But I wasn't going to let him speak just yet. "Don't. Just don't. We've all been worried sick about you, and they would've carted you back to wherever, tortured you some more, and kept you for as long as they felt like it, then killed you. So don't tell me that you can take care of yourself. This isn't normal criminal stuff. They mean business, Will. They have no mercy. If you want proof of that, I'll rip my chest open, and you can see what losing your parents at fourteen does to your heart. You're one of the most capable agents here—we get it—but one witch can't stand against this organisation. And we're not going to let you try. Like it or not, you're stuck with us looking out for you." I folded my arms and glared at him.

He pressed his lips together, his cheeks pink. There was obviously a lot he wanted to say, but he was holding back. James jumped in before he could unleash. "I hate to say it, but my sister's right, Will. None of us could stand up to these bastards by ourselves. The fact you even survived to make it back is a testament to your grit. You have no idea how valuable your intelligence on this organisation is. We can't afford to lose you for that fact alone. This isn't all just because we think you're a cool dude." James smirked.

"And," said Ma'am, "if I let anything happen to you, I'd never hear the end of it from Lily. I have to live with her, and she's rather moody when she's unhappy. You wouldn't wish that on Olivia and me, would you?" Even I smiled at that. Insult or not, if it helped Will make peace with this outcome, I was all for it. *Insult me some more!* "I've already arranged somewhere for you to stay. It's the safest place I could find. You'll only have to stay there for a week or two, so it won't be a terrible inconvenience. I don't want to hear any more about it. That's an order, Agent Blakesley."

Will raised a brow at me, then turned to Ma'am and shook his head. "You know I won't argue with an order." His defeated tone hurt my heart. But a sad, living Will was way better than a dead one.

Ma'am nodded. "Right, that's settled. Once Will's written his report, James and I will prepare our reports for this group, and we'll reconvene. I expect that to be in a couple of weeks. To sum up what's happened over the last few weeks, Regula Pythonissam has defrauded over one-hundred people in Westerham and surrounding villages. They convinced owners to sell their homes at a ridiculous discount by pretending to haunt their houses. The homes were sold to various companies, and all the victims are non-witches. We've managed to trace all these companies back to one parent company. The company is registered in Monaco, and from our initial enquiries, the owners are ghostlike themselves. All names and addresses seem to have been falsified. We believe by apprehending three men over the last few days, we've managed to curtail their fraud around Westerham, but we're currently in talks with other Bureaus about whether they're targeting other locales. Will has some information on their motivation, which, I'm sure you'll all agree, is disturbing but gives us valuable insight into Regula Pythonissam." She looked at Will. "Please tell everyone what you know."

He nodded. "I won't go into all the details of my assignment from the beginning, but I rarely had contact with anyone important in the group, except for one man, the one I was forced to kill two nights ago at Ma'am's neighbour's house. His name was Joseph Matteo Franco. He was close to Dana and might have been in Regula's inner circle. He headed up the scheme to buy properties cheap. Their goal was to build wealth, but that isn't all. They wanted to make non-witches suffer, put them in their place. It seems to be one of their manifestos. They're trying to move properties from non-witches to witches and impoverish non-witches in the process. They want subservience. My summation from listening to Franco talking to his buddies is that their overall goal is to out witches and have non-witches as the enslaved population. They consider witches to be superior, and they're sick of being 'in the shadows and forced to hide.'"

My brother's jaw muscle bulged, and he gripped the tabletop. The anger pulsing off him was palpable. It matched my own. *How dare they!* This was extreme racism. Yes, witches were human and not a different race to non-witches, but I didn't know what else to call it. Maybe magicalism?

"What about Oliver and Samuel? They weren't witches. Why would they help disempower their own kind?" They'd both seemed like decent people. I didn't want to believe they'd betray their own for money. Then again, it shouldn't surprise me. People did it every day.

"I can answer that," said Will. "They didn't know Franco was a witch. They were given addresses for leads, then offered more commissions to sell the houses to the companies. For every property they sold to—in effect, Franco—they would get another one to sell. Oliver cottoned on that the houses were all haunted after talking with the desperate owners, and he thought it was unusual. He started asking questions, and that was the end of that."

At least they hadn't known exactly what was going on. "But they still broke the law by convincing the owners to sell to Franco's people. Those properties weren't sold in an open market. They took advantage of people's distress to get their hands on more work."

"Money talks, unfortunately," said Imani. "Surely this can't be news to you, Lily."

"No, unfortunately it's not." I sank back into my chair. The world was such a crappy place sometimes. For the second time that day, I wished for the impossible: that people could just be nice to each other.

James straightened his already-straight tie. "We're working on getting some kind of compensation to the owners, but because we're having trouble tracking down the real new owners of the properties, it's going to be delayed. Once we work out the true identities of the three men we arrested, we'll confiscate any assets we can and use that to help pay back the victims."

Well, that was something. My gaze was drawn back to Will. It was so good to have him back. But it saddened me to see him running his hands nervously up and down his thighs. The furrows in his forehead were deeper than ever, and there was no sign of his cheeky dimples. How long would it take him to find his smile? He caught me watching him but then quickly averted his gaze. Sorrow flooded me, but I wasn't going to go under. I'd rise above it and take Will with me. We'd get through this together, no matter what it took.

Ma'am's voice rang out, steady and certain. "The last thing I want to say before we leave is that the things Will did while imprisoned by Franco and Regula Pythonissam were forced on him. It was comply or die. I'm sure we can all agree, Agent Blakesley has made incredible sacrifices to survive and provide us with information we desperately need but couldn't have gotten any other way. The PIB has pardoned him for any crimes committed in the pursuit of justice. Thank you for your service, Agent Blakesley."

Will raised his head and stared at Ma'am. His eyes shone with tears, but his voice didn't waver when he said, "Thank you. It is an honour to serve."

Ma'am stood. "To wrap up, Olivia will get back to work now, James is going to return tomorrow afternoon, and the rest of you can have a week off. Will and Lily, please stay. Everyone else, I'll see you later."

Liv threw me a perplexed look and wished me luck before she left. Was I in trouble again? Or did Angelica want to make sure I didn't lose it when Will finally told me that we couldn't be together? He wasn't the type to have asked for backup though. Despite laying down the law earlier, he was one of the strongest people I knew. If he found something tough, you knew it was something that would break lesser mortals.

Angelica walked over and sat in Olivia's chair. "I know you two haven't had a chance to talk things through yet, but my solution for where you're going to stay still stands. You're coming to stay at my place. I've had Beren put extra protections on the property. It's the only solution I'm happy with. I don't want any of you out of my sight, to be honest, not until we have a handle on what's going on. We came too close to losing you, Will, and I won't let it happen again."

Oh my God. He was going to live with us? What fresh hell was this? Living with a man I couldn't have. Thanks, universe. Talk about cruel.

"That's all I wanted to say. I'll leave you two to talk. I'm sure you have a lot of catching up to do." Her smile was gentle as she stood. Hmm, and how was it that no one had interrogated me about my new witch skills? Maybe no one had wanted Agent Bradford to know, which made sense.

Once the door had clicked closed behind Angelica, Will turned to me. We stared at each other for a minute, my heart trying to reach the speed of light. This was it. The moment I'd been dreading for weeks, since that moment at the bus stop in the rain. I swallowed.

He reached out a hand and gently ran the back of it down my cheek. His gaze softened. He shook his head slowly. His voice was gruff when he said, "God, how I missed you."

My nose tingled with the burn of tears. "I missed you too." I wanted to say so much more, but missing me didn't mean he wanted to get back together. And I'd let the L word out yesterday too. Everything was on the table. Maybe he'd forget, and we could pretend it wasn't out there making everything a bazillion times more awkward than it had to be.

"Was it my imagination yesterday, or did you say you loved me?" A little more blue glowed in his eyes, as if the clouds were parting.

My cheeks heated. Okay, so we weren't going to pretend I hadn't said it. "Yes, I did. I'm sorry, Will, but that's how I feel. It's okay if you don't feel the same. So much has happened since our fake break-up. I'm afraid it was actually real. It will break my heart if it was, but I'll be okay. I promise. And I still want to be here for you. If nothing else, I want us to be friends. I'll always care about you, I'm afraid."

He laughed. "Don't look so happy about it." He moved his chair closer to mine and leaned forward. "For your information, I do not want to break up with you, and here's something that might just surprise you: I love you too." The clouds parted all the way to reveal brightness as strong as the sun. His dimples were back! I grinned.

"You're not just saying that to make me feel better?"

"When have I ever done that?"

"Never?"

"That's right, and I'm not about to start now." He took my hands in his and stood, pulling me up with him. He wrapped his arms around me and gathered me close, then leaned down and kissed me. The zing of adrenaline careened around my body, making me light-headed, filling me with joy. His lips were warm, oh, and so was his tongue. Hmm, too much information, I'm sure.

As we kissed some more, I flicked the universe a thank you. It didn't always get it right, but when it did, it couldn't get it more right. The next two weeks were going to be amazing, and I wasn't going to waste a minute of it.

Will and Lily were back. Maybe we needed a couple name… Willy? Ah, no, maybe not.

Will's voice came through into my head. *Shut up, Lily, and just kiss me.*

ABOUT THE AUTHOR

USA Today bestselling author, Dionne Lister is a Sydneysider with a degree in creative writing, two Siamese cats, and is a member of the Science Fiction and Fantasy Writers of America. Daydreaming has always been her passion, so writing was a natural progression from staring out the window in primary school, and being an author was a dream she held since childhood.

Unfortunately, writing was only a hobby while Dionne worked as a property valuer in Sydney, until her mid-thirties when she returned to study and completed her creative writing degree. Since then, she has indulged her passion for writing while raising two children with her husband. Her books have attracted praise from Apple iBooks and have reached #1 on Amazon and iBooks charts worldwide, frequently occupying top 100 lists in fantasy. She's excited to add cozy mystery to the list of genres she writes. Magic and danger are always a heady combination.

If you want to find her on social media, click on the icons below.

ALSO BY DIONNE LISTER

Paranormal Investigation Bureau

Witchnapped in Westerham #1

Witch Swindled in Westerham #2

Witch Undercover in Westerham #3

Witchslapped in Westerham #4

Witch Silenced in Westerham #5

Killer Witch in Westerham #6

Witch Oracle in Westerham #8

Witchbotched in Westerham #9

The Circle of Talia

(YA Epic Fantasy)

Shadows of the Realm

A Time of Darkness

Realm of Blood and Fire

The Rose of Nerine

(Epic Fantasy)

Tempering the Rose

Printed in Great Britain
by Amazon

77749763R00154